ISBN 978-0-259-48412-7
PIBN 10819311

1 MONTH OF
FREE
READING

at

www.ForgottenBooks.com

By purchasing this book you are eligible for one month membership to ForgottenBooks.com, giving you unlimited access to our entire collection of over 1,000,000 titles via our web site and mobile apps.

To claim your free month visit:

www.forgottenbooks.com/free819311

English
Français
Deutsche
Italiano
Español
Português

www.forgottenbooks.com

Mythology Photography **Fiction**
Fishing Christianity **Art** Cooking
Essays Buddhism Freemasonry
Medicine **Biology** Music **Ancient
Egypt** Evolution Carpentry Physics
Dance Geology **Mathematics** Fitness
Shakespeare **Folklore** Yoga Marketing
Confidence Immortality Biographies
Poetry **Psychology** Witchcraft
Electronics Chemistry History **Law**
Accounting **Philosophy** Anthropology
Alchemy Drama Quantum Mechanics
Atheism Sexual Health **Ancient History**
Entrepreneurship Languages Sport
Paleontology Needlework Islam
Metaphysics Investment Archaeology
Parenting Statistics Criminology
Motivational

UNDER
SUMMER SKIES

BY

CLINTON SCOLLAD

With Illustrations by Margaret Lande Randolph

NEW YORK
ARLES L. WEBSTER & OMPANY
1892

UNDER SUMMER SKIES

BY

CLINTON SCOLLARD

With Illustrations by Margaret Landers Randolph

NEW YORK
CHARLES L. WEBSTER & COMPANY
1892

G
470
C

Where'er my pilgrim path has lain,—
Italian slope or Syrian plain,—
Wherever I have pitched my tent,
In Orient or Occident,
Still have I heard from friendly lip
The cheer of kind companionship.

To those who shed, in other days,
Their sunlight on the alien ways,
Who gave to joy a keener zest
Through sympathies—half unconfessed,
In green remembrance would I bring
These records of my wandering.

CONTENTS.

Contents.

Through the Streets and Bazars of Cairo with Dragoman Hassan.

UNDER SUMMER SKIES.

I.

THROUGH THE STREETS AND BAZARS OF CAIRO WITH DRAGOMAN HASSAN.

GOOD fortune is surely attendant upon the Egyptian traveler who falls in, at Cairo, with Dragoman Hassan. If at first the sleepy dullness that a greater part of the time seems to lurk within his eyes does not prepossess one in his favor, after a little it will be discovered that this veils a keen clear-sightedness very protective to him in whose behalf it is exercised. Aside from the peculiarity of his eyes, Hassan's face is distinctly attractive. A small drooping mustache curves above a sensitive mouth. His smile is like an illumining flash; the contour of his profile is indicative of a re-

13

finement few Arab faces show, while his broken English is simply delicious. Hassan is a good Mussulman. When he is busy piloting tourists through the mazes of the City of the Caliphs he cannot go to prayers five times a day, but he will assure you that at night he tells beads enough to make up for the day's shortcomings. To see Cairo under the guidance of one of "the faithful" opens the stranger's eyes to things he would not else observe, and makes the paving of many otherwise difficult paths easy. So, in the kindly recollection I hold of Dragoman Hassan, let me, before speaking further of him, a little after Oriental fashion, "bless his prayers."

With the attendant genius whom I have thus introduced, I found myself threading the Mousky, Cairo's main thoroughfare, one warm mid-winter morning. Life was at its flood. No gay carnival was ever more bewilderingly brilliant than the kaleidoscopic scene we looked upon. Babel could not have been more opulent in the noise of tongues. The donkey boys and camel-drivers shrieked "*Uh, ah! uh, ah!*" and with but small success in clearing a path ; sellers of lemonade, with their huge long-necked bottles carried by a strap slung over the shoulder, clinked their metal cups ; money-changers at their tiny stands rattled their piles of copper coins ; and there were cries innumerable from all sorts of pedestrian venders who momently escaped disaster as by a miracle. We beheld strange and often tempting-looking sweetmeats; sometimes borne above the head upon a great tray; sometimes offered for sale on a small three-legged table, over which the merchant waved, with frantic swoops, a many-wisped switch made of fine slits of palm leaf, to scare away the swarming flies. " Confection, O sugar for a nail, O confection," rose the appeal to the candy-lover. Sweets in exchange for a piece of old iron ! A man labored past us bearing a deep basket nearly filled with lemons. Behind him was a companion straining under the same weight of oranges. "God will make them light, O lemons ! " shouted one. " Honey, O oranges, honey ! " was the other's constant exclamation.

One of the most characteristic figures in Cairo's streets and bazars is the water-carrier. All day long he toils for a mere pittance, wandering hither and yon, bent nearly double under the weight of his uncouth, often dripping, bulging water-skin. Usually he cries out as he goes, " May God recompense me." At the time of Mohammedan feasts, charitable folk frequently hire these water-carriers to dole out water free of charge, and sometimes accompany them upon their rounds. When this occurs the carrier turns occasionally to his patron and exclaims, "God forgive thy sins, O dispenser of the drink offering ! "

As we were passing from the Mousky toward the drug-bazar, there came a loud shout from behind, and Hassan quickly said, "Your right side, sir." I sprang from the middle of the street, where I had been walking, and a richly dressed man, mounted upon a fiery, gayly-caparisoned Arab steed rode by. This was thoroughly illustrative of a certain street custom. No native pretends to move from the portion of the highway where he is walking unless particularly addressed by driver or rider, consequently there is a continual chorus of cries such as the following: "Your foot, lady!" "Your back, O chief!" "Your left side, O woman with the carrots!" ."Your right side, O man with the figs!"

Shopping in an Oriental country is not a thing to be lightly undertaken. In the first place, even if you are attended by a trustworthy guide, you are likely to be cheated. He is the cleverest merchant who can succeed in getting the most out of the European or American. You never dream of paying more than half the price asked (this, of course, when dealing with natives), and usually a bargain begins by the offer of one-third of the sum demanded. Words are poured out in a gesticulative stream by merchant and customer; and though you at first be an interested on-looker, such absurd palavering every time anything is bought becomes extremely wearisome. One feature in the Eastern system of purchasing, the lover of coffee does not find so objectionable, and that is the

custom of inviting purchasers to be
seated upon little low chairs, often
placed about, or upon the bazar divan,
and serving the dark-brown, thick Turk-

ish coffee in diminutive cups.   This frequently precedes a trade.

   " Cross-legged like a Turk," has be
come a proverbial expression.   Up and
down wherever you go in Oriental cities
such is indeed the attitude in which you
find the shop-keepers seated.   Often-
times so small are the little dens in

which they carry on their traffic that all of their stock, save that upon the very top shelves, can be reached without moving. They seem like dreamers, many of these merchants; and as they sit smoking their long dark-stemmed water-pipes (*nargileh*), they are the personification of indolence. When a tradesman is a good Mussulman, and wishes to go to prayers, he simply draws a net across the front of his shop (there are no door-ways), and takes his departure without further ado. At certain hours many of the bazars are quite deserted, but no one thinks of disturbing aught, such is the honor among these people whom we look upon as " heathen."

Hassan led me through the shoe-bazar without pausing. Overhead, stretched upon thin poles, were strips of sackcloth and of reed and palm matting to shield from the sun. Hanging on all sides, in streamers and festoons, were the pointed red and yellow slipper-shoes so largely worn. We encountered, now and then, a wandering dervish who resembled a walking rag-bag. Women brushed past with babes astride their shoulders,

Their dark eyes were " like stars above the dusk of their veils."

At last, after turnings that seemed unending, we came to the street of the book-sellers. Books, bound and un-bound, were piled about in the most distracting confusion The disorder, however, had an artistic side. Men of learned air were gathered in groups, no doubt holding wise converse. The non-intellectual loiterers paid no heed to us until we paused, and Hassan attempted to purchase a Koran. Then a crowd instantly gathered. The merchant flatly refused to sell, scowling at me the while and muttering curses on " Christian dogs." The loungers jeered audibly, and Hassan flew into a passion, as he could do when he deemed that occasion required. His passion had the desired effect, and we were not further molested. Our second attempt was no more successful than the first, although we were politely treated, but the third trial proved fortunate, and after the usual haggling, I marched triumphantly away with my Koran, bound in fashionable red.

The bazars of the perfumers and of the gold and silver smiths are labyrinthine —sinuous passages in which the stranger, if unattended, would become inextricably lost. Scanty light sifts in through occasional rifts in the improvised roofs, and in and out threads an interminable crowd of buyers and sellers, against whom it is impossible not to jostle, so narrow is the way. Hassan began bargaining for some attar of roses with a smiling young merchant, who was surrounded by bottles containing "all the perfumes of Araby." He vended the aromatic essences in slender, uniquely-fashioned vials that held but a few drops.

When our purchase was concluded he said "Good-bye" in English with such a funny upward-turned inflection that I found myself trying to reply in his own coin of adieu. It was curious to see the artisans in gold, silver and copper, to observe the primitive bellows employed by the forger, and to note the fine work the carver managed to accomplish with the rudest of tools.

As we wended hotel-ward my eye fell

upon some prayer-carpets displayed for sale.

"Could I buy one of those?" I said to Hassan.

"Why not?" returned he, in his queer way. "Yes, you buy."

We approached the proprietor of the establishment—if so large a word may be applied to so small an affair—and inquired prices.

"He want six francs; you give him two," explained Hassan, French being the medium of coinage that most foreigners employ.

Finally for two and a half francs I became the possessor of the coveted article, and now, should I ever desire to turn Mohammedan, I can at any moment resort to Mecca, for upon the prayer-carpet, in red, orange, purple, and consecrated green, is figured the holy mosque of the Prophet and the sacred palm-tree that stands at its side.

II.

The Dervishes.

II.

IT was high noon at Cairo. A merry party had come out from a bounteous lunch in the dining-room of the Hotel du Nil, and was gathered about a juggler who was showing his skill in the "black art" near a pavilion that stood in the center of the lovely garden. Opening upon this charming tropical bower, palm-studded, set with brilliant bloom, were the rooms of the guests who were abiding in the two-storied, balconied cottages. Quite apart is all this from the dense life of the Egyptian capital city. You reach the hotel by a narrow, uninviting passage-way, and come upon its delightful plot of greenery unexpectedly. At night, when the Orient moon is shining, the place has an almost divine enchantment.

The juggling was over. Chickens had

25

appeared and disappeared miraculously, rings had been charmed into playing fantastic pranks, and a baleful cobra had moved to and fro upon the stones to a weird tune from the lips of the conjurer. Word was passed that the leisure hour was at an end, and we hastened toward the Mousky, and the carriage that there awaited us.

Soon we turned sharply into a narrow and nameless side-thoroughfare, from which debouched dim windings of various bazars. People stopped and stared as if a circus were passing, and we in turn continually gazed at what was to us a never-ceasing show. Before a low archway we alighted. Following our guide, we traversed a small dusty court between tumble-down buildings, that presented an indescribable picture of neglect, descended a short flight of worn stone steps, and entered by a cramped door-way a diminutive-domed mosque.

The building was circular in shape. Upon its ceiling were grotesque frescoes —passages from the Koran inscribed in inter-wreathed Arabic characters. Into the gallery above only "the faithful" were admitted, and there were many groups of old and young awaiting, with seeming stolidity, the hour when the holy ceremonies should begin. We were allowed to enter a narrow space outside a low-railed octagonal inclosure, where, upon finely-braided reed matting, near the railing, a number of dervishes were sitting. A few moments passed before all of the devotees appeared, coming from an inner apartment and gaining their places through a little back-swung gate. They were twenty-three in number. Their hats were of brown felt, and were tall and conical. Their over-gowns were of different subdued hues—red, brown, blue, and yellow—and dropped nearly to their feet. When the sheik shambled in all arose and bowed humbly. The sheik was patriarchal in appearance. His white beard hung down and spread fan-like over his breast, and his bent shoulders seemed to bear the oppressive weight of many years. Around his hat was a band of green, signifying that he had made the sacred pilgrimage to Mecca. At his death this emerald

honor-color will adorn the topmost
marble of his tomb.   Opposite the entrance gate-way he seated himself upon
a sheep-skin mat, dyed vivid crimson.
Eight musicians in a secluded portion
of the gallery now struck up a faint
monotonous tune, playing upon primitive flutes, and beating drums that might
have belonged to a pre-historic era.
Slowly all the dervishes arose, the sheik
with them.   One by one they passed
the place where the sheik had been
seated, pausing to bow twice profoundly.
Most of them had cast aside the loose
socks they wore on entering.   Three
times they glided around the inclosure, then the sheik resumed his mat,
and the music quickened.   Outer robes
were now cast aside, and each devotee
stood revealed in a long, wide, white
gown girt at the waist.   The upper part
of this garment from the neck down
was embroidered with fine threads of
gold.   One stepped from the matting
toward the center of the polished wooden
floor, extended his arms, and began to
whirl, using one leg as a pivot.   His eyes
were nearly closed.   One palm was up-

ward lifted to signify heavenly aspira-
tion, one was inverted to denote a yet
unbroken allegiance to the best influ-
ences on earth. Each in turn took up
the dizzy spinning. Their garments,
which soon filled like bellying sails,
never touched as they spun faster and
faster upon their bewildering round.
The musicians began a measured singing, and an aged dervish in a purple
robe walked among his fellows, not
coming once in contact with an extended finger-tip nor the hem of an
outflying skirt. All the while the
sheik remained sitting with closed eyes,
now and then swaying his age-bent body
backward and forward. This was to them
religious ecstasy. They sought to sep-
arate the soul from the body, to render
themselves so insensible to the affairs of
the world that they might commune
face to face, being to being, with the
divine power. The exhibition (we could
scarcely apply any other term to what
we saw) had for us a wonderful fascina-
tion ; there was nothing revolting
about it, nothing profane. Their motions had a poetic rhythm, and yet when

we emerged into daylight from the dim-
ness, the monotony of sound, the eccentric sight, we felt our heads eddying,
and not until we were plunged into the
excitement of a race toward the spot
where stranger scenes were to be enacted,
did we lose the distressing sensation.

On the verge of the city, in the midst
of blinding white dust-clouds we halted.
The heat was stifling. We sank ankle-
deep in powdery particles as we plod-
ded toward a building whose round
roof was just visible above grouped huts
of mud. Through a dark vestibule we
gained a circular room, smaller than the
one we had just left, but in other respects
similar. There was the same shaped
dome, the same peculiar characters upon
the wall. In the middle of the apartment, seated upon dark mats outspread
upon the floor, were eighteen men.
Among them was a boy of twelve. The
eldest had snowy hair, and was a fine
type of manhood. They were dressed
in vari-colored bright gowns. As we
entered, while still seated, they began a
dolorous chanting. This ceased, and
they rose slowly and were silent for a

moment. One of their number now faced the group. At an almost imperceptible sign they commenced to utter low cries, that gradually increased in power until the sound seemed like the ominous growling of a pack of mongrel curs. The effort shook the frame until every muscle quivered painfully. This came at length to an end, but almost immediately they essayed a different form of emotional expression. They panted like exhausted animals, slowly at first, but anon with greater and greater force, swaying their supple bodies backward and forward, loosening their long silken hair, that was tossed and flung in dusky streamers about their faces. Now clashed in the din of huge tambourines, the bass of a drum, and the sudden sharp note of the cymbals, while piercing above all rose the shrill treble of a hideous, giant black, who stood in one corner of the room, with head thrown back and cavernous mouth wide agape. Suddenly the pandemonium of noise died away. Perspiration stood in great beads upon the brows of the dervishes ; yet, gasping though they were, they allowed themselves but an instant's respite. One, whose motions and cries had been most violent, stepped from the half circle and took the place of the leader. Now, with a sidelong yet graceful movement, still timed by the discordant beating of the musical instruments, the weird and awful worship was continued. Prolonged howls, disjointed shrieks, issued from the lips of the men upon whom frenzy had seized. Every instant we looked with growing apprehension, expecting to see one or more of the number fall upon the floor and writhe in convulsions, as so frequently happens. Momently the scene grew more frightful in its intensity, the barbarous noises swelling, the eyes of the dervishes dilating, their limbs shaking as if with palsy. The grotesque element we at first found had vanished. It was horrible, and we made as precipitate an exit as we dared.

Somewhere I have read that in the olden time, in the early Mohammedan days, the noblest men, among them the Persian poet Hafiz (he of the roses and the tuneful nightingales), belonged to these ascetic brethren. No one who broadly observes can deny that there have been high thinkers among the followers of El Islam, but to-day the leaders of lofty intellect and inspiring example are no more. We see little now save the emptiness, the exaggeration, the distortion of a form of devotion which the founders of the sect and its early members, invested with great spirituality. It is but the barren husk that held the vital grain.

III.

*By Night and by Day in the City
of the Caliphs.*

III.

BY NIGHT AND BY DAY IN THE CITY OF THE CALIPHS.

LONG since had the last muezzin-call echoed above the house-tops. Into the single tapering garden palm-tree a marauding owl had come for a night's shelter, and the round moon of the Orient, undimmed above, was shining gloriously for some Egyptian Endymion. The piano in the open-air music-room was silent; every one was moon-gazing. Wafts of warm breeze blew occasional scraps of conversation and trills of laughter across the bowery inclosure, and no jarring noise was borne in from the great city that had not yet sunk into slumber. Upon this ideal evening scene there suddenly broke a weird, discordant, mournful sound that caused the laughter to die upon the lip and brought conversation to an abrupt close. Every one listened intently. The melancholy

37

wail rose louder, fell, rose again, and was prolonged into a kind of shout.

A hotel porter was passing, and some one hailed him and inquired the cause of the unearthly disturbance.

"An Arab whose home is near by has died," he said, "and they are mourning for him. You may be able to see them if you go to the roof of the hotel."

All were familiar with the promenade upon the hotel-top, and there was a general stampede. Up the stairs we flew in a manner which, when reflected upon, appeared decidedly unseemly. Yes, the porter was right. Some fifty or sixty feet almost directly below, in a small court-yard, we could see distinctly, in the brilliant moonlight, eight or ten long-gowned Arabs dancing up and down around a white donkey, with clapping of palms and disconsolate cries. Periodically the donkey brayed in sympathy. They were hired mourners, we were told (donkey and all, mayhap), for the deceased had been a man of both wealth and position. When one party of wailers was exhausted, another took its place, and upon learning that this interchange would continue far into the small hours of the night, we were inclined to wish ourselves a little farther removed from the preparatory obsequies.

How truly Oriental the scene was !— the ghostly minarets reeling in the moonlight, the flat house-tops with shadowy forms upon them, the inky silhouettes of the scattered palm-trees, and then the extraordinary sight below, that had its pathetic as well as its grotesque side.

As we descended, a young Englishman, fleshy and florid, came rushing in, his eyes gleaming with excitement.

"Oh ! I say, I *have* had a time," he cried to us, swinging his arms wildly ; "I went around to the funeral, and they chased me away. My, but I wish another Arab would 'kick' so that we could have a repetition of this." He was so agitated that he knew not what he said ; but when he appeared the next morning with a bottled scorpion, he declared, solemnly and calmly enough, that the creature had been frightened from its native haunts and scared into scaling the mosquito netting that encompassed his bed by the heathen orgy over the dead Arab.

The grand door-way of the mosque of the Sultan Hassan is a masterpiece of Saracenic architecture. It is lofty and imposing, and yet so fine and lace-like are the arabesques surmounting the gracefully carved arch that one is more impressed with the delicacy of its form and outline than with its grandeur. However small or unpretending a mosque may be, no one is allowed to enter it shoe-shod. Slippers must be worn, or one may go stocking-footed. For the convenience of visitors a supply of huge, flimsy slippers of cloth and flexible leather is kept at the shrines most frequented. These may be slipped over the shoes and tied loosely. In this wise one morning we entered the mosque of the Sultan Hassan, and shuffled over the great marble-paved court-yard like so many wide-footed dromedaries. The fountain in the center of this inclosure, built of colored marbles, ("the faithful" here performed their ablutions before praying), must have been a marvel of beauty in Cairo's palmy days, but now it shows only a shadow of its former loveliness. From the fountained court four lofty alcoves open, forming a cross. In one of these were a number of devotees bowing toward Mecca ; in another a boy was sweeping the rush matting with a huge broom of slit palm leaves. Suspended from the roof on all sides were long ropes and chains. At the time of the fast of Ramadan, lamps are attached to these, and by night the mosque presents a unique spectacle. Within a lofty domed chamber the Sultan Hassan lies buried in splendid state. He was a renowned monarch, and was regarded as beneficent in his time. It was a mark of his large-heartedness, I suppose, that when he saw how beautiful a mosque the architect had erected for him, he cut off the servitor's hands, lest an edifice more stately should be fashioned for some rival prince.

Mohammedan places of worship bear to one another a great similarity. The style of architecture varies but little ; there are always the fountains for ablution, meaningless arabesques that become desperately wearisome (the religion allows the figuring of nothing that resembles the human form or that of any creature), and inscriptions from the Koran, not particularly edifying even to those versed in Arabic characters. Yet if one can overlook the general likeness, there will always be some detail that will interest,—an exquisite mosaic, fine inlaid work of ivory or mother-of-pearl, Persian carpets of unknown age, soft, wondrous of dye, and of exquisite pattern. Connected with many of the mosques, too, are interesting legends and strange superstitions. Suspended from the arch through which the sheik must pass to ascend the *mambar* (or pulpit) is usually a piece of carpet consecrated at Mecca, and it is said that buried under the slabs of marble in the holy recess of one of the mosques, are some of the garments worn by the Prophet. The oldest mosque in the City of the Caliphs is that of Amr, in old Cairo. Here is the famous pillar of gray marble marked with a spiral vein of white. The builder, Amr, desiring a column from Mecca, expressed his wish to the Sultan. This worthy monarch, whose name was Omar, being in the birthplace of Mohammed, commanded a column once and twice to depart for his capital beside the Nile. Finding the obstinate marble did not move, he struck it with his lash, crying as he did so, "I command thee in God's name, O column, to arise and betake thyself to Cairo!" On the following morning the column stood in the spot it has since occupied, bearing the mark of the Sultan's scourge.

The mosque of El Azhar is the largest existing Moslem university. In its courts, halls, alcoves, and recesses, eight thousand students from all parts of the Mohammedan world sit cross-legged, and con in their low monotonous singsong the Koran, and books on Arabic jurisprudence. Outside the main entrance, barbers ply their trade, shaving alike learned and unlearned crowns.

In seeking the " Red Mosque " (so called from its appearance), we passed the divorce court. Here the functionaries are kept constantly busy, for a man may divorce his wife by entering complaint and allowing her a ridiculously small sum per week for three months. The " Red Mosque " contains a pillar that is supposed to work a magical cure. If one is afflicted with a throat malady, half a lemon rubbed upon this pillar, and then eaten, will dissipate the disease—at least, so it is averred. We had come out of this lemon-bestrewn place, and were purchasing sandal-wood rosaries from an honest-seeming, bow-backed old Arab, when suddenly Hassan, who was acting as general utility-man, gave a savage shout, pounced upon a woman who had evidently crowded up to enjoy our trading, and raised his stick as though he would give her a sound beating. Some of us interfered, much to Hassan's disgust, and the captive was allowed to slink away.

"She bad woman," Hassan said ; "she try to steal from you," pointing to one of the party. "I no beat her now, but wait till I catch her 'gen." And he brandished his cane in a way that boded no good for the culprit should she cross our angered dragoman's path.

In the mosque-tomb of the Sultan Barbûk is a hollowed stone, to which tradition assigns miraculous properties. All infirmities are supposed to be cured by drinking water allowed to stand in the hollow. Some of us must have looked incredulous when we heard this statement, for a woman came forward and offered herself as a living proof of such a draught's healing power. She was a miserable, decrepit creature. Her skin was as wrinkled as a crumpled garment after a long journey, and, adding to the hideousness of her aspect, her unkempt hair had been dyed a bricky red.

Crowning the citadel, which the British red-coats hold with a firm hand to-day, is the alabaster Mosque of Mohammed Ali, whose slender minarets sentinel the city. In a narrow lane (the old approach to the citadel) the founder

of the present Egyptian dynasty had
the last of the Mamelukes executed.
The thrilling escape of one who leaped
his horse into the moat through a hole
in the wall, reads like a page from the
" Arabian Nights."   The spacious court
through which the visitor passes before
entering the mosque shines almost mirror-like in the burning sun, so polished are
the blocks of alabaster with which it is
paved, and when one crosses the dazzling
surface the effort is that of walking upon
ice.   The interior of the mosque is
effective, with intermingled cross-lights
and cool deep shadows.   Carpets as
soft as heaped wool, and as precious as
hoarded gems, cover the floor ; globular
glass lamps are suspended by chains
from the vaulted roof ; and in one corner, inclosed by a gilded grating, is
Mohammed Ali's sumptuous tomb.
There is a curious, square-shafted well
on the citadel heights, known as
" Joseph's Well," and really so called because the Sultan Yûsuf discovered it
while carrying on some excavations ;
but in spite of the acknowledged truth
of this fact, the story of Joseph and his

brethren is still vaguely and absurdly connected with it. We grasped candles, half slid down a dusty passage, descended a few steps of stone, and craned our necks to peer into the pit's fabled depths. Then we emerged to seek, in the rear of the magnificent mosque, a grand outlook that commands a wide sweep of the city roofs, a view of the palm-bordered Nile, with the slant *dahabeyah* sails, and beyond, guarding the approach to the brown waste of the Libyan Desert, the great Pyramids of Gizeh.

On the opposite side of the city, beneath its eastern wall, Burckhardt, the famous Oriental traveler, is buried in an unknown grave in a dilapidated Moslem cemetery.

Somewhere beneath old Cairo's walls he lies,
　Around him resting forms of alien clay,
And o'er him leaning his loved Orient skies,
　Bright with eternal summer's fervid ray.

Where camels pass in broken, laggard lines,
　And wretched curs prowl dumbly for a bone,
Ah! little recks he how the sunlight shines
　Athwart the green that crests his burial stone.

Thus have the Moslems honored him, 'tis said—
  Believing in their blessed faith he died—
By placing proudly o'er his fallen head
  The vernal hue Mohammed sanctified.

For his worn feet the hallowed soil had trod
  Of Mecca the belovèd; and the soul,
They deem, will win the straightest path to God
  That seeks on earth the holy pilgrim goal.

Better his tombèd dust should tarry here
  Than 'mid the Alpine snows where he was
    born ;
His nature kept its summer through the year—
  His heart turned ever steadfast toward the
    morn.

IV.

Round About Cairo.

IV.

SHOUBRA AVENUE, with its arching acacias, is the fashionable drive of Cairo. It was our good fortune one morning to ride down this shady highway to the entrance of an extensive orange grove, owned by a kindly young pasha, whose name I should certainly record as a benefactor if I but knew it. We were allowed to wander among the fruit-goldened trees, and to feast our fill on blood oranges and sweet lemons. Then we made a pilgrimage to the Boulak Museum, in the village of that name. Here is a glorious prospect for an Egypt-ologist. Sarcophagi, mum-mies (veritable Pharaohs), idols ("Ye giant shades of Ra and Tum"), and hiero-glyphics without end. Would it be dreadful heresy to con-fess that, after gazing long upon the relics of past ages, I found the wide

51

sweep of the Nile, the slant-sailed boats, and the opposite line of stately palms, as seen from the broad-walled embankment near, vastly more engaging?

Heliopolis is a pleasant excursion from Cairo. This was the city of the sun and the city of obelisks. Over the spot where it stood the white-bloomed Egyptian clover now waves. But one of its stately monuments remains. Central Park in New York, Thames Embankment in London, squares in Berlin, Rome and Constantinople tell of the pride and splendor of dead Egyptian dynasties. Near the one remaining obelisk we found a patient ox turning a great water-wheel, which sent a clear and copious stream to irrigate the flowering fields. Here, by the flowing water, beneath a tamarisk tree, an Arab sheik had spread his prayer-carpet, and was devoutly bowing toward Mecca. Children gathered about us and begged pleadingly, following far along the dusty road as we whirled away, to be pelted with small coin, very fractional in value.

Although no one pretends to believe

the legend in regard to it, nearly all visitors to Heliopolis pause at the " Virgin's Tree," a scarred and hoary sycamore standing in a garden about half a mile from where the obelisk rises in solitary state. Tradition has it that during "the flight into Egypt" Mary and the infant Christ rested beneath this sycamore. It is recorded, however, that the present tree is but about two hundred years old, having been planted shortly after the death of the bole that formerly flourished on the spot. We had a draught of pleasantly cool water from the Virgin's Well, which gushes plentifully near at hand. That this is authentic is not an impossibility, for in such a country a running fountain would have been prized and tended from the time of the first inhabitant.

Within the confines of old Cairo is a curious Coptic village. A fragment of ancient wall partially surrounds it, and admittance is gained through an entrance guarded by a massive wooden door. A primitive yet ingenious lock secures this ponderous relic, and a swarthy porter stands on duty to open

and close the barrier. The key he
wields is of wood, and is as formid-
able as a bludgeon.· The streets here
are merely laneways ; a loaded camel
could not traverse them. The upper
windows of many of the houses are lat-
ticed. Those dwelling opposite, if sitting in these windows, could easily
shake hands with one another.

We descended a sand-hill in stifling
dust and heat, and, having entered the
precincts of the Coptic town, found its
shadow and coolness delightful. In an
open spot not far away a Moslem fair
was in progress, for it was their Sunday
—Friday. Without there were booths
and gay crowds, minstrelsy and the
magic of jugglers. Here was pensive
quietude, with only a faint and far-away
murmur of the festivity. A pleasant-
faced guide went before us, and the
omnipresent Hassan brought up the rear.
In passing a dark entry we heard
the unintelligible jumble of many voices.

"What is going on in there ?" we inquired of Hassan.

"It is a school," he said. "You like
to see? Come! "

We followed him along the passage-way, from the end of which a ray of light glimmered. A sudden turn brought us into a tiny court, where a dozen bright-eyed boys were squatting cross-legged around an intelligent-look-ing young man. Each boy had an Arabic Bible, and they were reading in concert. Our advent produced a trans-formation scene. They sprang to their feet and clustered about us, books in hand. They began reading glibly, and now and then we caught a few words of English. After a little they paused, and then chorused, their eyes glittering, their white teeth gleaming, *"Bakshîsh!"*

The Coptic church of St. Mary, built upon the site of the house where Christ and his mother are said to have dwelt while in Egypt, is interesting aside from its traditional note. The peculiar wind-ing entrance-way, the nave of the church, with its strange screen divisions, the crude antique portraits of the saints, the mosaic work and fine carving in ivory, the tiny crypt with its sacred niche and baptismal font, in which, ac-cording to the Coptic ritual, the babe to be baptised must be three times **im-mersed**—all, together with the rapt air of our attendant, combined to take us back to the early days of Christianity, and brought vividly to our minds the vicissitudes of those who, in those troublous and uncertain times, embraced the faith of the Nazarene.

The day appointed for our excursion to the great pyramids dawned with a jewel sky—flawless Egyptian sapphire. We had given up the idea of making the trip on donkey-back, and, seated in a comfortable open conveyance drawn by two stout horses, with Hassan, looking more wide-awake than usual, upon the box, we crossed the lion-guarded bridge that spans the Nile and sped along the fine, shaded roadway that leads toward the desert's edge. Long lines of laden camels were moving leisurely city-ward. We paused a moment at an orange market by the roadside and purchased for the merest trifle all the fruit we could comfortably carry. Then we drove merrily on. As we approached the looming bulk of the giant pyramid, after a ride of about an hour, lean Be·

douins, who had been loitering by the way, pursued us, shouting : " You climb the pyramids ? You climb the pyramids?" They were provokingly persistent, one fellow following us nearly a mile, until Hassan seized in despair the driver's whip and made so mad a lunge that our tormentor thought best to relinquish the chase.

The sun beat down scorchingly as we left the shady avenue and drew up in front of a small, square house of stone, erected for the use of travelers, not far from the Pyramid of Cheops. A throng of Arabs instantly gathered about us, and after a short consultation on the part of Hassan with their sheik, three of these grinning, jabbering creatures were assigned to each one of us, and with them we approached the steep mountain which we were to climb. The ascent was to be made at the nearest angle, there being at this point a little more regularity in the huge blocks of stone. One Arab seized each arm and one took his station behind to push. In this order our procession started. Holding in mind the story of the man who kept crying to his attendants, "*Yallah, yallah,*" (which means faster), when he meant to say, "*Swoyeh,*" (slower), and hence arrived at the summit in an almost unconscious condition, I admonished my guardians at the outset, and halted occasionally to catch the ever-widening view. What a panorama lay outspread when we reached the summit! Before us lay the broad, green river-belt, with its grain fields, its palms and its villages; there was Cairo, with its sun-brightened roofs and domes, the minarets of the great alabaster mosque of Mohammed Ali towering majestic above all; behind us, in its billowy desolation of brown, swept the Libyan Desert; dotting the southern distance were the Sakara and Dahshûr groups of pyramids; and nearer rose, enigmatic from the sand, the head and shoulders of the Sphinx.

If one wishes to be nearly suffocated, to be dragged and hauled up, down and along black passages by two Arabs, to have the satisfaction of gazing at the blank walls of a contracted stone chamber, in the center of which is an empty sarcophagus—in short, if one desires to become generally uncomfortable and to appreciate fully a breath of pure air and the sight of the undimmed sun, let him explore the interior of the Pyramid of Cheops. Having had a surfeit of exploration, I perched upon a convenient

block of stone and awaited my companions, who were still buried in darkness. While there seated, an Arab approached me and addressed me in English. He had a rogue's face, and proceeded to reel off the greatest number of falsehoods I had ever heard in so short a space of time. He was worse than a nightmare. I purchased one of the *curios* offered me by this modern Ananias, not to reward his crookedness of tongue, but to rid myself of his importunities. The image of

Isis I thus acquired, seems to be always upon the verge of speech, and should its oracular lips ever open I shall expect to hear it spin, in emulation of its whilom owner, astounding yarns of the long-dead days in which it was worshiped.

As we walked towards the Sphinx across the burning sand, we were met by an Arab with his camel. " Ho ! for a ride," we all exclaimed. The man's palm was crossed with some small coin and we mounted and rode one by one. Each time the beast was made to kneel he groaned and moaned distressingly ; each time he rose it seemed to the person in the saddle as if he were going to be shot far into the heavens ; and all of us declared, when we were again pacing *terra firma*, that our respective spines felt as if they had been bent and snapped like whip-lashes.

About half a century ago an English officer discovered, not very far from the Gizeh Pyramids, a large walled shaft, some twenty-five feet in depth, at the bottom of which, imbedded in rock, was a black marble sarcophagus. This has since been called Campbell's

Tomb. As we passed it, an Arab clambered down and scraped the sand away from the sarcophagus. Before our coming, this wily son of the desert had piled it up there. The Arab, like the " Heathen Chinee," has " ways that are dark."

A few moments later we were standing before the Sphinx. In front of this gigantic statue the sand has been excavated, and the paws, brick-built, have been laid bare. Here an altar once stood, and hither we clambered down,

and looked up sixty feet at the gigantic
scarred face. What name had they of
yore for this divinity, those ancient
Memphians? What celestial personality did they reverence through this
semi-human image? To whom offer
sacrifices? To whom bow down in worship? Still the riddle of the ages remains unread, and the lips of stone smile
on immutably at our vain conjectures.

V.

Sixteen Miles on Yankee Doodle.

V.

SIXTEEN MILES ON YANKEE DOODLE.

YANKEE DOODLE was the name of a donkey that I selected from twenty or more of his kind just outside the railway station of Bedrashên. I chose him for a certain sagacity which I fancied I discerned in his countenance, and for his intelligent ears. His master rejoiced in the name of Mehemet. He was an Arab boy, with sparkling dark eyes, a voluble tongue, and a pair of legs most remarkably nimble. It was the last day in February that I bestrode Yankee Doodle, and with Mehemet running in the rear, armed with a long piece of dried sugarcane, started off at an easy lope for Sakara. To leave behind the mud huts of Bedrashên did not take many strides, and I soon found myself traversing a winding embankment which makes the route passable during the time of the

65

Nile inundations. Below, lay fields of white-flowered Egyptian clover, and green reaches of ripening barley.

"Him good donkey," Mehemet averred, as my Arab steed was urged into a gallop by a prod from the end of the sugar-cane. After several abrupt leaps, caused by the same unkindly appliance, I came to the conclusion that my Nubian whip of rhinoceros hide, for which I had searched Cairo bazars, would be more judiciously used upon master than upon beast, and Mehemet speedily found that it was wise to keep at a distance. After this little understanding between us, all went well.

We passed lazily moving camels, their riders teetering backward and forward, while often a number of the ungraceful animals went by, heavily laden with white clover which was fastened in huge bale-like bundles upon their sides. We made our first halt in a grove of palm-trees, upon the site of ancient Memphis, by the side of a recently discovered statue, which bears a striking resemblance to the figure of Ramses, that lay so long face downward in the mire and sand. Of the forgotten splendor that was Memphis, the mute lips of these colossal statues speak more forcibly than all the weighty tomes of an army of Egyptologists.

Having galloped across a shadeless plain, I reined Yankee Doodle in the shadow of a village mud wall, and a horde of dirty children gathered around and shrieked, "Bakshîsh." They were very scantily clad, these children of the sun, and the garments they wore made one desire to keep them at a goodly distance ; but they had bright, pleasant faces, many of them, and when a smile lit up their dusky countenances, there was a flash of sunshine on disclosed pearl. Through palms, upon which the sand had encroached, I now took my way, and erelong emerged to ascend a slope that led westward toward the Libyan Desert's heart. Now the sun began to beat down blindingly. Mehemet lagged, and I raised my umbrella-roof. For more than an hour I threaded the ups and downs of the dazzling, scorching waste, and then, upon a cragged hill's broken crest, where rough steps de-

scended to a portaled tomb's entrance, I
halted. Opposite, white in the glare of
the heat, stood the great step pyramid
of Sakara; adjoining were smaller
kingly sepulchres; and far away northward the massive piles of Gizeh notched
the sky with their keen triangles.

Of all the tombs in the necropolis of
Sakara, that of Pthi is the most perfect
in decorative beauty. It is a delight to
leave for a time the blank expanse of the
desert, to go down between walls that
the sand ruthlessly drifts over, to enter
cool passages and follow a small taper's
flickering flame, and finally to see, il-
lumined by a sudden flare of magnesium
wire, the walls of the marvelous underground chamber. Here, in ordered row,
are pictures finely fashioned, represent-
ing the various arts at which man toiled
in the days when Egyptian civilization
led the world. You may see the sower,
the reaper, men following cattle at the
plow, the baker placing loaves in the
oven, the fisherman, sailors in ships
wielding serried banks of oars, the car-
penter, the smith, the hunter and his
hounds, and folk engaged in many other

occupations. There are traces of color upon these curious designs that all the added ages have not wholly obliterated.

Remarkable though such tombs may be, it is upon the Serapeum that the greatest interest centers. The avenue upon which, from both sides, lines of sphinxes looked, and along which, at later times, the statues of Greek poets and philosophers were placed, is now a vale of sand, from which here and there peep dismantled pedestals and columns. Only by constant excavation is the entrance to the Bull Pits kept clear from the burying element. Here were the sacred animals brought and entombed after life was extinct, and they had been worshiped during the allotted period in the Memphian temple. Here, too, in chapels, all traces of which have disappeared, did men, forswearing intercourse with mortals, live out ascetic lives, devoting themselves to the rites of Serapis. In huge granite sarcophagi the bodies of the bulls found final rest. Threading the vaulted passages of the Serapeum to-day, the flutter of innumerable bats will affright the ear. At regular intervals are chambers cut from the solid rock. Here the sarcophagi repose. In past ages, no one can say when, these massive coffins were all broken into by sacrilegious hands, and some long hidden treasure was doubtless discovered and borne away.

Can imagination picture with what strange ceremony each holy bull was entombed? Whether by night or day, the same torches must have flared aloft. Priestly devotees, perchance, carried the inanimate bulk; weird, wild music resounded through the ghostly corridors, and mournful voices were heard in solemn chant. How many centuries the desert winds have wailed their triumphant dirge since then—the dirge for Memphis dead! Yet these tombs, that were the abode of death, have outlasted all, and remain to typify not death but life to us.

At the house erected by an explorer, Mariotte Bey, to whom all praise is due, Yankee Doodle lunched, Mehemet lunched, and I lunched ; then we turned our backs upon Sakara, and hastened toward the emerald line with which the Nile cuts Egypt.

The Egyptian buffalo is a grotesque-looking creature. It has a hide that is a deep grayish brown, upon which little hair grows. It has horns that curve down and outward. It has, too, a stubborn head and an ugly eye. Yankee Doodle was fond of a gallop, and was indulging in one along a pathway just above a field where three buffaloes were feeding. They cast malicious glances upon my steed, upon Mehemet running near, and without seeming to pause for consultation, bolted after us. Mehemet's exit from the scene into an adjoining clump of palms was most precipitate. I descried a line of advancing camels not far ahead and brought my goad into active use. Yankee Doodle took in the situation, and we were away, while the angry creatures came snorting on behind. It was not a long chase, for just before we reached the camels the buffaloes sheered off into the fields, and without further incident, Mehemet having come up, we passed Bedrashên, and hastened on to the Nile.

We gained the river. Moored near at
hand were many clumsy river-craft. I
left Yankee Doodle in Mehemet's charge

and embarked, with some
twenty-five others, in one of
the rough, single-masted,
huge - sailed boats. The
order was given that every
one should be seated, and
that no one should stir
until we arrived at the opposite shore. The sides of
our vessel were almost
upon a level with the wa-
ter. It seemed as if a single
flaw in the breeze would
tip us all into the dirty
green of the stream. We
sighed and resigned our-
selves to Providence. At
first we appeared to scarcely move, then the sail
slowly filled, we heard the
water begin to ripple, and
the broad prow of our *dahebeyeh* dashed
up white particles of spray. Our landing
was safely effected, and how ungrateful
I should be had I aught but agreeable

things to say of a boat that carried me safely across the sire of rivers. My auxiliaries soon arrived, and over an unpicturesque plain we rode to the baths of Helouan. There I bade adieu to Mehemet, and to Yankee Doodle, not without a bestowal of ample "Bakshish," and an affirmative nod at Mehemet's parting words: " *Him good donkey.*"

We gained the r
hat were many
left Yankee D

VI.

On Horseback in the Land of the Philistines.

VI.

ON HORSEBACK IN THE LAND OF THE PHILISTINES.

VERY early one March morning I was wakened from sound slumber by what seemed a miniature pandemonium just at my ear. I started upright, and found myself upon a narrow iron bedstead, in a tent whose lining pictured to my astonished vision fantastic arabesques.

From another cot near by, my comrade
was gazing about with the same look of
bewildered amazement my countenance
doubtless showed. Then, in a flash, it
all dawned upon us. We were in camp
at Jaffa; and the remarkable aggrega-
tion of sounds that had so suddenly
roused us—a bell, a horn, a pair of tin
cymbals—was our dragoman's rising
signal.

Let me introduce our dragoman,
Demetrius Domian. He was a Greek of
about thirty—tall, stalwart, a sort of
bronzed Apollo, if you will; and he sat
his horse as gracefully as Alexander bestrode Bucephalus of old. He was a
capital linguist. His Arabic sounded
poetic, and his English was at times irre-
sistibly quaint. In fact, he proved himself to be " an all-around good fellow."

There was not a cloud in the sky to greet
us that first morning, and the sirocco
that had parched us when we landed the
day previous had been tempered during
the night by a northern breeze. Camp
breakfast was a jolly affair, as we sat
upon our canvas stools, around the improvised table, in the large dining tent.

From the outset we had nothing but good words for our cook. He was a culinary prince, and constantly surprised us with tempting morsels.

At seven o'clock, the horses were ready, and the tents had been pulled down and packed, together with our baggage, upon the mules. A few moments later, and we were prepared to start. Our steeds, without doubt, were strangely assorted. Each animal had some eccentricity; and, as we stood regarding the creatures, we could but smile as we thought of the figure we should cut. And yet we found that it was no laughing matter. One animal bit, one shied, one bucked—all kicked. This was at first. The charger which had been assigned to me I speedily christened Bruté. He was white. A portion of his mane and tail had been cropped, and I judged that he had been troubled with fatigue from his birth. This was a mistake on my part; for, later, I ascertained his latent powers— that he could go at a tremendous pace. Furthermore, I found him to be unusually docile—for a Syrian horse. He

never offered to bite, and only kicked
when some brother steed tried to take a
generous nibble from his already scanty
tail.

For an escort we had a Turkish soldier
named Mustapha, and a gorgeously ar-
rayed individual he was. His *kaffeyeh*
(head-dress) was black. He wore a blue
jacket, trimmed with gold braid, over a
waistcoat of very dark red. His wide
trousers were white, and were tucked
into the tops of cavalry boots made of
some kind of embossed leather. His
eyes were like twin deep pools, silvered
by moonlight ; and his black mustaches
made a double bow. Between escort
and dragoman we were in picturesque
company.

From our camping-ground we crossed
a Mussulman burial-place to gain the
road. It was a forlorn, weed-grown spot.
The unique tombstones were often
neighborly, tilting toward one another
at every conceivable angle. We threaded
slowly through the crowded market-
square toward the Jerusalem highway.
Camels, horses, donkeys, men and
women, closely pressed about improvised

booths and bazars; and there rose an
unintelligible jargon. Golden heaps of
well-nigh seedless Jaffa oranges tempted
us, and soon we found ourselves riding
between orchards whose trees bowed beneath the weight of the juicy oval fruit.
We turned shortly from the post-road
into a bridle-path, and commenced our
journey southward over the plain of
Sharon. On both sides the land was
gently undulating. The fields were
green with grass and young wheat, or
purple with the thick bloom of the
lupine. Anemones lighted their tiny
torches along our way, and an occasional
tulip lifted a thirsty cup. During the
morning we encountered stray Arabs
astride diminutive donkeys, and descried laborers plowing, sometimes
with an ox, sometimes with a camel,
using always a most primitive plow
that looked at a distance like the crooked
root of a tree. This implement was
made of two pieces of wood, roughly
fastened together, and demonstrated to
us more plainly than almost anything
else could have done, how dead mechan-
ical ingenuity is among the present tillers

of holy soil. On far slopes appeared black Bedouin tents that seemed like huge bats with outstretched wings.

Toward noon our attention was attracted by grass-covered conical pro-tuberances, pointing upward like a series of huge ant-hills from an eminence upon our left. We did not discover until we were quite near at hand that this was a town—Yebna. People came out to welcome us, and gathered around the spot where we paused for luncheon, under some decrepit olive-trees, at a judicious distance from their abodes. They were wretched specimens of hu-manity—the men wolfish, the women stolid (if one chanced to catch a glimpse of a female face), and the children imp-like. We found it restful to stretch out upon the carpets provided for us ; and our steeds, evidently envious, endeav-ored, whenever they were not watched, to emulate our example. Bruté was the first to roll.

Before we finished our noontide repast, our camp mules filed by. An iron bell, worn by the leader, jangled as do the bells worn by cattle on Alpine heights.

We lazed about nearly two hours more ; and then " Horseback, please," one of Demetrius's warning cries, was heard. It was pleasant riding that afternoon across the undulent, flower-studded plain, with a cool breeze blowing over the sand-dunes that a few miles away stretched along the shore of the Mediterranean. We crossed a deep-banked but dry-bedded water-course, by a curious yet well-preserved Roman bridge, the first thing indicative of civilization, ancient or modern, we had seen since leaving Jaffa. The sun was still quite high in the heavens when, passing through a laneway bordered by cactus hedges twelve feet in height, we rode into Ashdod, and found, beyond the mud huts that constitute the town, the friendly white of our tents. The sheik, with his patriarchal beard, followed by a cringing throng, came out to offer us greeting.

" Marhaba " (welcome), he said, with the Eastern salutation, touching with his right hand his lips, forehead, and heart. It was a strange reception.

Our horses were cared for, guards

were placed to keep the thievish natives at a distance, and we set out through the narrow streets, vile with dirt, for the eminence where the Ark of the Covenant is supposed to have rested when captured by the Philistines. At first we had a troop at our heels ; but, when our pursuers saw that we were bent on climbing, they gradually dropped away. It was a very brief ascent, however—a tiny though rather steep hill, that afforded us a fine view of the squalid, windowless habitations beneath us, of the green sweep of surrounding country, and of the far-away blue reaches of the Mediterranean. Scrawny curs appeared upon the thickly thatched house-roofs, and barked at us as we descended. A rough wooden door, that opened into a mud-walled court, was ajar ; and our curiosity overcoming our prudence, we peered in. Two houses were entered from the straw-strewn enclosure ; and in the door-way of one sat a haggard, wrinkled woman grinding corn between two stones, the one hollow, the other round. Beholding us in the gateway, she uttered a startled cry and veiled her face, as though she had been a bashful maid of sixteen, whereat we deemed it wise to withdraw. That night an Arab caravan encamped not far from our place of tenting ; and, as we wandered about in the starlight, we could see shadowy forms clustered around a cheerful fire.

Birds were singing merrily in the cactus hedges the next morning when we mounted. Through a vista of fig and olive trees we beheld a black-robed woman standing in a statuesque pose beside a water-wheel that a sleepy ox was turning. She did not so much as move her head while we were riding by ; and her form became a silhouette upon my memory. It must have been quite mid-morning when we traversed a long stretch of cultivated ground, and struck into a path leading directly toward the coast. We now had visible proofs of how the sand, inblown from the shore, is encroaching upon this fertile region. We crossed great brown drifts of it, from which oft-times peeped the dead topmost branches of a fig or olive tree. Finally, after many windings, the path brought us to a small village, where we procured a guide, who led us at a brisk trot through narrow lanes between thriving orchards. Suddenly, after ups and downs that seemed interminable, we came out below a great bulk of ruined wall, vine and flower and grass overgrown. We sprang from our horses, and clambered up a fragment-strewn acclivity. Then, standing in the Jerusalem gateway of Askelon, we looked upon the desolation of one of the great " cities of old time." Sand-drifts had scaled the remnants of the southern wall, and choked the harbor ; a riotous

tangle of shrub and vine and rank grass
obscured every trace of habitation ; the
sea spread out its shimmering sapphire
expanse beyond ; and behind, where our
horses were tethered, was the spot where
the tide of many a battle had surged to
and fro. Helmed Christian and turbaned Moslem had flashed sword and
scimitar in the same bright sunlight that
goldened this peaceful yet desolate scene.
Herod the Great was born here, and in
the time of his power adorned the city
with gardens and colonnades. Here
Richard Cœur de Lion fought, and the
mighty Saladin.

Leaving Askelon to its final fate,
complete obliteration by the sand, we
rode through the heat of the day Gaza-
ward, and, passing venerable olive groves,
came to that town, with its girdle of orchards and its crown of palms. It was
not a difficult matter to find the way
to the principal square, facing which
stood the governor's residence, and a
dilapidated fortress, used as barracks,
where some sullen-browed Turkish soldiers were lounging. Among them Mustapha found an acquaintance, whom he

ardently embraced. His excellency, the governor, having kept us waiting a long time, was not inclined, when he did appear, to grant us the desired permission to visit the grand mosque. In fact, he regarded us with suspicion, until one of our party, seeing the state of affairs, produced a Turkish passport bearing some magic words—the general "*open sesame*" of a high functionary in Constantinople. Instantly there was a change in the demeanor of the governor. He saluted all of us smilingly. He was delighted to think we had honored the city with our presence, the old hypocrite!) He would provide us with an escort to visit the mosque at once. And soon we were following at the heels of one of the sullen, ragged privates.

The mosque was interesting from an antiquarian point of view. It had formerly been a Christian church ; and the still remaining marble columns showed the debased Byzantine style of art. Above the spot where the altar once stood, a scimitar had been marked in gilt upon the white-washed wall, emblematic of Mohammed's conquest by the sword. A class of boys, seated cross-legged about a white-bearded instructor, regarded us curiously as we passed them, mumbling the while their lesson from the Koran. We left the rough slippers we had been obliged to wear over our shoes, at the entrance door, and, having visited a number of small, though richly stored bazars (particularly those of the fruit merchants), we retreated to our camp, which was pitched in an open field below the town. Mohammed's grandfather is buried at Gaza, and "the faithful" affirm that the bones of Samson repose there also. They keep the building containing his tomb religiously closed, however, as though they feared his remains might take upon themselves to walk abroad and repeat the destruction that he is here said to have wrought while in the flesh. The "top of the hill that is before Hebron," whither the lusty hero is reputed to have borne the gates of the ancient city is to-day pointed out—a tomb-covered crest, to the south of the town. Beyond this, the desert stretches away blankly to the horizon. The sky was aglow with sunset fires that evening, and Gaza's palms and minarets stood in black outline against the vivid background.

Our third day on horseback put all of us into the merriest spirits. We began to grow accustomed to the little eccentricities of our horses; and the vigorous exercise already had a bracing effect upon our appetites. During the night the elements had indulged in a hearty frolic, and miniature lakes dotted the low-lying ground. The air was purer for the rain; and we saw that the distant atmosphere had cleared, as we rode over the green billowy hills toward the purple Judean mountain country. We had a number of sharp races that morning, and for the first time I discovered Bruté's latent accomplishments. Everywhere the "lilies of the field" uplifted their slender stalks, and cloud-shadows of varied shape made beautiful the slopes of new-plowed red loam. For hours not a tree met the eye; and, when we paused for luncheon near the mud village of Falujeh, our only shelter from the scorching sun was a cactus hedge. From a deep well near by, women were

drawing water, which they bore away
in earthen jars, gracefully poised upon
their heads. On squares blocked out
upon a sandy spot, two venerable Arabs
were playing with black and white pebbles at a game which seemed like
checkers. The town urchins became too
curious several times, and gathered
about us in a constantly narrowing
semicircle, which Demetrius found it
necessary to break somewhat forcibly.
It was amusing to see the scattering
when he brandished his long-lashed
goad.

That afternoon our pathway led over
stony slopes, and Mustapha was in his
element. His horse was a splendid
animal, and together they executed some
clever cavalry maneuvers for our en-
tertainment. It was the young Syrian's
particular delight to dart over a rocky
field at full gallop, leaning back in his
saddle, and whirling his gun wildly
above his head, then to wheel suddenly,
and charge upon an imaginary foe, his
weapon sighted as though in act of
firing.

The sun was sinking low and the air

growing chill, as we rode down a valley, and saw, beyond the rising ground where our tents were pitched, the Arab town of Bêt-Jibrin, identified by some as ancient Gath, Eleutheropolis of the time of the Roman supremacy, and as Gibelin of the era of the Crusades. When we appeared, on the following morning, Demetrius greeted us with a smile and his usual friendly handgrasp.

"We caught a thief last night," he said.

" A thief ! " we chorused. "What did you do with him ? What was he trying to steal ? "

" The muleteers gave him a good thrashing ; and he is now in the kitchen tent, guarded by Mustapha," our dragoman replied. " We captured him in the center of the camp, creeping on his hands and knees. He said he was looking for his donkey." And Demetrius gave one of his hearty laughs at the manifest absurdity of the culprit's excuse.

We strolled toward the kitchen tent to have a look at the marauder, who proved to be harmless enough in appearance, save for a hangdog cast of countenance. He was attired in sack-cloth, and wore a pair of shoes that might have served the " old woman " of the nursery rhyme. When we struck camp he was set at liberty, with a part-ing admonition from the lash, which Demetrius insisted should be bestowed upon him.

At Bêt-Jibrin are the remains of two Crusade churches, a ruined fortress, and a fragment of moated wall. To the caves, however, that honeycomb a hill adjoining the town, the principal inter-est attaches. Theories have been ad-vanced that many of these excavations were originally dwellings, and later turned into storehouses for grain. There is no doubt that the more modern of the caves were intended for and used as *columbaria*, since cinerary urns can still be seen in niches that line their walls. The fact that they are modeled after the vaults upon the Appian Way, in Rome, indicates that they belong to the Roman period.

Supplied with torches and attended by two Arab guides, we filed up through flourishing olive groves brilliantly aflame with the scattered bonfires of the anemone. A long, stony slope where goats were browsing was next crossed, and we dismounted to peer through irregular openings into the many-niched *columbaria.*

The crest of the hill was gained on foot, the muleteers taking charge of our horses. A short distance below the summit, at the base of a precipitous incline, was the entrance to the ancient caves. The two Arabs descended with catlike agility, and Demetrius followed. We craned our necks and looked down. The prospect was not an agreeable one. There were fifteen feet of moist perpendicular wall, with scarce a foothold, and then fifteen feet more of débris, sharply declining into intense blackness, that led we knew not whither. We were not discouraged, however, and, one by one, with the assistance of those below, we safely effected the descent. The torches were then lighted and our under-earth wanderings began. Now stooping to avoid some cragged projection, now crawling upon hands and knees, now clinging closely to the wall on the edge of a black gulf, we went deeper and deeper into the abode of night. Often our path was intersected by two or three passages. Colder and colder grew the air.

"Be careful!" came a warning shout from Demetrius. Singly we entered an oval doorway, and stood upon the brink of what appeared to be a yawning pit. Into its depths wound a narrow spiral stone stairway. We flattened our bodies close to the wall, clung to little projections, and crept downward. A misstep meant that which we shuddered to contemplate. Finally, in safety, we stood upon the floor of a spacious and lofty conical chamber. On the walls were the marks of the tools with which it had been hewn out, how many thousand years ago no history can affirm. We started to seek daylight by a different path from that of our descent, so that we might visit another of the subterranean rooms. Suddenly those in front halted, and we heard Demetrius's voice: "This wretch of an Arab says he *thinks* he knows the way," he called out to us. Then there came a series of explosive utterances, prefaced by an expression with which we had grown familiar. Demetrius had called one of the guides " the son of a pig ! " The cavernous passages wildly echoed the angry cries, until it seemed to every one of us as though there was a chorus of unseen fiends gibbering in our ears.

The guardian spirit of our party seized Demetrius by the arm. " For heaven's sake," he said, " if you want to quarrel, wait until we get into the upper air. If those fellows should put out the torches, a pretty predicament we'd be in!"

Our dragoman was impressed with this advice. " That is a good idea," he returned. Then he addressed the Arab in that individual's vernacular, which is as rich in epithets of esteem as it is in curses.

" O my brother," he said to him, " we will trust in you; we will follow in your footsteps. Lead the way, O knowing one ! "

Peace was restored, and ere many moments we beheld a welcome gleam of day. I think no one of us ever hailed the kindly sunbeams more thankfully.

We shall not soon forget, I am sure, the
caves of Bêt-Jibrin.

When we turned our backs upon ancient Gath, we left Philistia behind ; but
we had by no means seen the last of the
Philistines. A revolver discharged by a
reckless hand at an impudent cur barking
from a Zakûka house-top brought an in-
dignant crowd after us ; but we speedily
distanced our angry pursuers, and raced
on into the heart of the Judean mountains, where the fragile maiden-hair fern
and the pale pink cyclamen peeped
gracefully from rocky clefts. We wound
up through a wild defile to an eminence
whence the Mediterranean was visible,
and then rode downward to Hebron,
nestling amid its orchards, passing as
we went the leafless vineyards of Eschol,
where the fabulous grapes are grown.
Fanaticism has its abode at Hebron.
Boys surrounded and stoned the camp.
We walked to the entrance of the great
mosque (further no Christian is allowed
to go), escorted by four of the garrison
soldiers, two in advance and two in the
rear. We were called " sons of pigs,"
" children of the devil," and our prayers

were cursed by the Frank-hating popu-
lace. That night camp guards were
doubled ; and the next morning, having
cast farewell glances at the lofty twin
minarets that tower, according to Moslem tradition, over the graves of Abra-
ham, Isaac and Joseph, we set joyful
faces toward the kindlier walls of Beth-
lehem, and broke into a swinging gallop
that rapidly bore us far northward.

VII.

A Night at Jericho.

VII.

A NIGHT AT JERICHO.

We had ridden in the early gol
dawn down from the rugged desolat
of the Judean wilderness to the sh
of Bahr Lût, the Dead Sea. Its silv
expanse swept southward before
clear and mirror-like. Gray and gr
the mountains of Moab loomed abov
eastern bank, the full flood of mid-mc
ing light upon them. A line of vi
green in the predominant sultry brc
marked the delta of the Jordan, wh
empties through two mouths. The cr

103

tal water of the sea was tempting, and we bathed. To feel ourselves floating about like so many corks was delightful indeed. The longing to participate in a really good plunge was strong upon us, but prudence forbade such an indulgence. Woe betide the venturesome wight who dips his head in the Dead Sea! His hair will be clotted with salt, his eyes will burn, and, if he chance to swallow a few drops of the bitter brine, he will think a river of molten lead is coursing through his vitals. There was no breath of air stirring as we turned our backs upon the deceitfully clear water and the wide bow of beach. The sun had mounted nearly to the zenith ; our horses were fagged ; and we crossed the parched plain toward the Jordan ford, a thirsty and drooping caravan.

Our handsome Greek dragoman led the way. Behind him came the sheik of the Jordan Valley and his servants, who were our escort. One of these servants was a lean Nubian, above six feet in height. His skinny legs, protruding from his long dark robe, looked like blackened pipe-stems. He carried a huge, old-fashioned Arab gun, the stock and a portion of the barrel of which were bound with strips of brass. Behind this advance-guard rode the party, the " Guardian," as we styled a young Englishman who was accompanying us, bringing up the rear. The latter was versed in Eastern tongues and Eastern ways, knew Palestine much better than many parts of his native land, and was pluck and joviality personified.

He who has always pictured to himself the Jordan as being a lovely, limpid stream, purling between flowery banks, must be undeceived! It is little more than a large, turbulent, muddy creek, lined by a tangle of vines and shrubs, in many places wholly impenetrable. Above rise bare bluffs of clay, brown and sunscorched. Grateful, indeed, to us, however, was the shade of the little willow grove in which we found ourselves, after having followed for some moments a sinuous and narrow path through matted undergrowth. The water rippling among the graceful reeds was as musical to listen to as the most crystalline of Arcadian fountains. Birds, gay of plumage, trilled in the over-arching boughs, or darted across our arc of vision like detached bits of a rainbow. Strips of carpeting were unrolled, and luncheon spread. We did not find it too hot to eat, but to move, after our repast, seemed impossible. So we leaned back and day-dreamed ; and, seeing through half-closed lids the broken beams of gold flicker upon the reeds, we wished for Pan and his satyr troop to come and pluck and tune them to some drowsy woodland melody.

"Go to Jericho!" How often had we been thus exhorted! And now we were on horseback, and going. Never need we be told again to make the pilgrimage!

The noonday heat began to be tempered by a mountain-born breeze blowing down from Galilee and the snowy slopes of Hermon. Gaining higher ground, we came upon a field where twenty or thirty camels were grazing, their drivers being nowhere visible, having probably crept into hollows, or hidden themselves behind dwarf balsam-trees to escape from the full force of the

sun. After a time, the green that em-
bowers the cluster of mud hovels that
form the modern Jericho became less
blurlike ; and at length we passed the
white walls of the Russian Hospice, and
halted in an open space in front of a
deserted building which bore, in staring
great letters, this sign, " Jericho Hotel."
On the tops of their huts and· upon the
summits of adjoining refuse heaps, the
wretched inhabitants had gathered.
There were half-naked children in
swarms, women who partially veiled
their faces with their dark gowns, and
men who appeared stolid and indiffer-
ent. About a mile distant we found our
tents pitched on the supposed site of the
ancient city. To reach our camping-
ground we wound between gardens
where flourished bananas and figs, and
then through thickets of thorn-trees.
We forded the stream called Ain-es-
Sultan (this is " the healed fountain of
Elisha "), and paused at the spot where
it gushes clear, and in strong volume
from the base of a rocky hill. Nearing
camp, we saw the gum-arablc plant and
the Dead Sea fruit, or apples of Sodom,

growing by the way. Above, in the distance, approached by a series of foot-hills, towered the so-called "Mons Quarantana," the Mount of Temptation, according to many authorities. Here, in the time of the Crusades, a monastery and chapel were hewn in the almost precipitous rock of the mountain side ; and even to-day one or two of the caverns are occupied by Abyssinian or Greek anchorites.

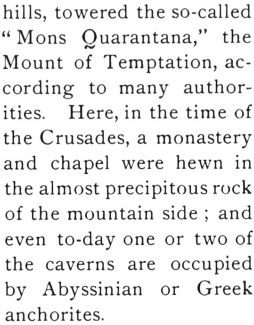

Our camp cook seemed to have put an extra touch upon his culinary efforts that evening ; and, while we were yet feasting, darkness dropped down suddenly. We strolled out into the little inclosure the tents made. The servants brought camp-stools, and placed them in a semicircle. Then from hidden stores two Chinese lanterns were produced, lighted, and hung upon armed posts driven for the purpose. We seated ourselves, and soon out of the darkness a strange band came forward.

There were men in long, loose robes of brown and white, wearing the graceful Syrian head-dress. There were women and girls in dark gowns, with un-bound, flowing hair. The latter stood aside, and the men joined hands, and began a low monotonous chant, bending their bodies backward and forward in time. Now they seemed almost to crouch upon the ground; now they rose to their full stature. At times, their chant was low and mourn-ful. At times, it swelled into a wild exultant cry. In front of the line, one who appeared of giant height danced

in swift gyrations, flourishing a gleaming scimetar above his head. Often, he
advanced with a demoniacal shout, and
waved his weapon in our very faces.
Knowing that he was merely endeavor-
ing to frighten us, we tried to present
an unruffled exterior, but found it a difficult matter, and were inclined to be
thankful when the men stepped back,
and gave way to the women and girls,
who began swaying their lithe forms,
clapping their palms and lilting a singsong air. There was a repetition of the
sword performance by two graceful
creatures, who threaded in and out with
rhythmic swaying of their glittering
blades. Next there appeared a man and
a boy, the one bearing a pair of primitive cymbals, the other a drum made of
goat-skin stretched over a frame of clay.
They played and sang, leaped and
grimaced before us; and then the whole
throng dissolved into the night as quietly
as they had emerged.

So intent had we been upon the grotesque performance of the natives that
we had not noticed the dark, ominous
clouds that had crept up the sky from

behind the mountain line. There was a portentous silence in the air, which was suddenly broken by swift, swirling gusts of wind, following close one upon another. Sand and fine pebbles were cast violently into our faces. Our canvas shelters shook, and the strained ropes creaked. We heard our dragoman shout to the muleteers, bidding them run for large stones to weigh down the tent fastenings. They dashed across the enclosure toward a rocky slope flanking the camp, where a great fire had been kindled. The wind had seized upon the brands, and they were capering, like so many fire-fiends, off into the night. A moment after the disappearance of the muleteers, we heard the murmur of voices in the vicinity of the fire. The murmur grew in volume, as does the sound made by a wave at sea, storming in upon a jagged coast. Broken, angry cries rose above the general confused clamor ; and, in the fitful light thrown by the dying flames, we could distinguish a dark, swaying mass of human forms.

What was happening? Had the

whilom dancers returned to plunder the camp? Were we being set upon by the Bedouins of the south, about whom wild stories had been told?

While we were conjecturing what could be the cause of the disturbance, and laying about us for such weapons as we could put hands upon, our friend, the " Guardian," sprang out of the dining-tent, dashed across the intervening space, and plunged into the thick of the *mélée.* An instant afterward, the sharp report of a gun cut the air, and a bullet made its fierce music in our ears. What a mad chorus of shouts followed! They seemed to come hurtling down the wind in menace. They were distorted by the blast into the laugh of the hyena and the howl of the jackal.

We were debating an advance, when the tumult began to subside. Then out of the still vociferous crowd stalked the " Guardian," bearing the large brass-bound gun belonging to our attendant sheik's Nubian servant. The young Englishman was panting and pale from exertion and excitement.

" Wait until I get my breath, and I

will tell you about it," he said. Presently, we learned the story. It seemed that, early in the evening, the Nubian, scenting the coming of a storm by desert instinct, had brought large stones down from the hill crest, erected a rude barrier near the fire, and spread some strips of carpeting within it. When the muleteers were commanded by the dragoman to fetch stones to pile upon the tent fastenings, they began to demolish the Nubian's shelter. This was too much for human nature to endure. The blackamoor cursed them in Moslem fashion,— cursed their ancestors and their own prayers. This failing in effect, he clubbed his gun, and savagely attacked them. Then the uproar began. On the appearance of the " Guardian," seized by a greater frenzy, the already furious man suddenly presented his weapon and fired ; and having fought desperately for the possession of it until overpowered, he took to his heels, and made off for the mountains. The wrangling of the muleteers over the gun was finally quelled, and the " Guardian " assumed charge of it. Then the sheik, who was

at first inclined to be angry, was paci-
fied. That night there was little rest.
The wind continued to blow with violence, and the dragoman said meaning-
ly : " It is well to be ready to move
on the shortest notice. The Nubian has
friends not far away. He *might* return."
This hint we all acted upon, throwing
ourselves upon our cots without removing
so much as a coat.

In the gray of a gusty, showery morning, we joyfully said adieu to Jericho
and the Jordan valley, and penetrated
the Judean wilderness once more. Toward noon we approached the squalid
village of Bethany, and shortly afterward
beheld the walls and towers of the Holy
City from a spur of the Mount of Olives,

A few days later, a strange scene
was enacted in front of the Jaffa Gate.
We had come up from the valley of
Hinnom, past the lines of kneeling
camels and the whining lepers, and were
about entering the city, when we beheld
the sheik of the Jordan and the dejected
Nubian coming toward us. The former
gravely saluted the " Guardian " after
the manner of the Orient, making a

motion to touch with his right hand his lips, his forehead, and his heart.

"I have brought my slave, that he may crave your pardon," he said. The Nubian dropped upon his knees and kissed the " Guardian's " feet, seized his hand, kissed it three times, and pressed it three times to his forehead.

" O chief," he cried, " I ask your forgiveness. Restore me to your favor, and return to me my gun ! "

" My brother," the " Guardian " replied, the colloquy being carried on in the poetic Arabic, " I treasure up enmity against no man. You might have killed me, but let it pass. I forgive you. The gun shall be yours again."

Thus we parted, going our different ways. The brass-bound musket was sent back to its owner ; and, doubtless, he shoulders it now, as he follows his master over the Judean mountains, or plods through the fierce heat of the Jordan Valley.

VIII.

Going by Gondola to Murano.

VIII.

GOING BY GONDOLA TO MURANO.

The golden light of afternoon
  Is bright on dome and tower,
And high above the broad lagoon
  The bells outclang the hour ;
They ring and ring in mellow chime
  · And echo far and clear ;
So while your supple oar keeps time,
  Row on, O gondolier !

Row on ! row on ! and leave behind
  The stately palace walls :
I long to breathe the loving wind
  That softly seaward calls,
To let the sands of time run out
  Like tides that ebb and veer ;
So put your graceful prow about,
  And row, O gondolier !

FROM the arcade upon the right of the Piazza San Marco a narrow-roofed passage leads to a cozy little *albergo*, where the table linen is freshly clean, where the waiters are remarkably polite, and where "good things" well-cooked, though not sold for a song, can at least be had at very reasonable prices. My fellow wanderer and myself had lunched sumptuously upon macaroni. When we reached the piazza we found it stewing in a dazzling afternoon sun. The Campanile cast but a slight shadow, the guides had disappeared from in front of the cathedral, and almost the only human beings visible were a few gondoliers, who were stretched in the shade of the pedestal, upon whose summit the lion of St. Mark spreads its never-furled wings. A breath of air, as heated as that of a furnace, sprang up from the pavement and scorched our faces as we hurried toward the arcade that stretches along the Piazzetta to the Molo. Gaining this friendly shelter, we sauntered toward the quay, where a long line of gondolas invariably lie moored. One gondolier, knowing by keen Italian in-

tuition that we were bent upon finding
the haunt of the breezes of afternoon,
suddenly roused from what had appeared
to be deep slumber, and approached
us without a trace of sleepiness in his
dark brown eyes. He was neatly attired
in the garb so many gondoliers affect—
a white linen shirt and trowsers, with
broad collar and cuffs of sailor blue.
His gondola proved an attractive one.
He doffed his hat to us with all the
grace of a mediæval cavalier, and we
hired him. He was Number Five; further
than this fact **his** personality was a sealed
book to us.

"*A Lido, Signori? Maggiore ? Reden-
tore ? Canal Grande ? Expozitione ? Murano ?*" queried our gondolier.

"Murano !" we exclaimed. "Yes, we
will go to Murano." And so it was
settled. Number Five seized his long
oar and we glided toward that canal
over which the Bridge of Sighs throws
its much-romanced-of arch. It is a picturesque bridge, and I know not why
some writers should take it upon themselves to pounce down upon all of our
pet illusions concerning it, unless it be

that they hold all illusions are bad for the soul. For our part we quite refused to be dis-illusionized, and continued to regard the grotesque heads that look down from it, and the windows that frame no more the passing prisoners' faces, until a turn in the canal shut it abruptly from sight.

How pleasant it was to wind through those narrow water-ways; past streets where the roofs seemed to lean and meet, and squares where the sun beat blindingly down on shop and church facade ; past other gondolas filled with the idle, handsome Venetian folk, and great, black, clumsy coal-barges poled by singing workmen!

Soon after San Giovanni and the Doge's tombs were left behind, we came out into the broad lagoon that shimmered, a wide stretch of lucent gold. There before us, a dismal blot upon so fair a scene, rose the hideous brick front of the Campo Santo. It remains an unsolved enigma, how Venetians, with a love of beauty that shows itself in nearly every line of their fair city, can tolorate this abomination of carroty wall. One is inclined to question whether the bones of the departed buried within the enclosure enjoy a peaceful repose. We were very thankful when our circle of vision embraced it no more, and hailed with pleasure the campanile of San Donato upon Murano, that soon towered into clearer view.

From a distance Murano partakes somewhat of Venetian picturesqueness. The campanile is graceful to look upon, the grouping of the houses seems not without artistic effect,and there are bits of green here and there to relieve the monotony of paint and tile and plaster. But Murano is the apotheosis of dinginess. In all the desert of uncleanness we discovered but one oasis, and that was a small square at one side of the cathedral. Our approach to the heart of the town was through a straight canal, bridged at intervals by spans of recent date and bordered by the most wretched looking wine-shops it had ever been our lot to behold. Those shops that were not for the open purpose of wine vending, had such an anomalous appearance that one is forced to include all under the single comprehensive title. To two glass-warehouses and the Museo Civico, however, exception must be made.

Murano has for centuries been the home of the Venetian glass industry, and at her factories the most exquisitely fragile articles are manufactured. How, out of so much filth such beauty can spring will ever remain to me a mystery. The warehouses had no charms for us, (we had just visited a wonderful display of glass in Venice,) but in an evil hour we were lured into the Museo Civico. I had already that day been led with lamb-like docility into one building so called, and I am sure it must have been during some temporary loss of my senses that I allowed myself to be persuaded to cross the threshold of this edifice that was all in a name. The only thing I have now to solace me for this mournful waste of time, is the remembrance of the profound bow the custodian of the place made to me, after I had bestowed upon him the princely sum of ten centimes!

I know not upon whose shoulders to cast the burden of the statement that San Donato rivals San Marco in the

stateliness and splendor of its interior.
Some mortal must have viewed Murano's
cathedral through glasses of peculiar
magnifying power. True, the floor of
each church is laid in mosaic of the
same character, but save for a certain
likeness in general form the similarity
here ceases. San Donato is in no respect
an attractive or interesting structure.
We could understand why, from a par-
tial sense of proprietorship, the verger
who showed us about should be enthusiastic over certain very ordinary paintings and frescoes, and a series of marble
columns erroneously said to be " Grecian
in style," but in his feeling we found it
impossible to share. We were much
more interested in the efforts of a young
and pretty mother to teach her toddling
boy to kneel and cross himself before a
crucifix, than we were in anything the
verger could show us.

From the well in the piazza near the
cathedral, of which I have already made
mention, four or five women and girls
were drawing water in shining copper
kettles. No doubt their sturdy hus-
bands and brothers were lolling some-

where in the shade, or were fast asleep
in wine-shop or upon cushioned boat
seat. These bare-headed, bare-armed
peasants were goodly to see, graceful
and deep-eyed and bronzed. They regarded our curious observance of their
water-bearing good naturedly, and no
doubt speculated among themselves
afterward who those crazy foreigners
were that wandered so aimlessly about
the sunny piazza.

There is no means of locomotion that
can be compared with the delight of
gondola riding. The lulling, side-long
movement that only suggests a swinging
hammock, the easy rhythmical gliding
through the water, the sound of the long
oar as it dips and turns and rises—all
combine in producing a sensation of
restful happiness that has no counter-
part. There is a buoyancy, an elation,
and at the same time a peaceful
dreaminess that transport one into that
realm, where the nine muses weave
their featsome dance with Apollo.

As we moved Venice-ward through
Murano's grand canal, the tide was
swirling seaward. Into its wildest eddies

did our pilot guide us, and we danced along like a bubble boat with a fairy at its helm. The sun was beginning to lessen in the west, and, as we emerged from the network of canals upon the Guidecca once more, we saw the dome of Santa Maria della Salute standing full in the spreading glow. Down the lagoon we motioned our gondolier, and where, black of hulk and ominous with hidden guns, loomed two huge Italian men-of-war, we turned and looked long upon the day's dying glory, and Venice pillowed on the sunset's breast.

IX.

.

Through the Streets of Bologna.

30

IX.

UNLESS churches be with one a hobby, Bologna's " interiors " will not hold anything of very marked interest ; but coming to the " city of arcades " from Venice, there will be much in its streets to arrest the eye of the southward-faring traveler. After the gay life that ebbs and flows in the Piazza San Marco, the first glimpse of Bologna, even though it be late some sunny afternoon, when the mid-day heat has been tempered by the breeze that anticipates evening, will not inspire an atom of that enthusiasm that so often thrills the breast of him who looks for the first time on Venetian water-ways. Yet when night has darkly

131

mantled the town, and a dinner of goodly viands, Italian-seasoned, has been eaten, sitting in a cool and clean court-yard with a square of still sun-touched azure above, there will come a kindly and sympathetic feeling.   The lights flashing beneath unending arcades, the crowd that has suddenly come forth to stroll and laugh and linger, the spangled heavens overleaning lovingly—all this will efface the sense of loneliness that massive buildings and highways little frequented are likely to impart.

It is a fortunate thing to see Bologna's leaning towers first by starlight.   They are a fine preparation for Pisa.   You may be inclined to think that the latter world's wonder can not be more unreal, more impossible, than the smaller of these two antique structures, reaching blackly heavenward.   It seems to be forever falling, and yet never meeting the shrinking earth.   There is a solemnity, an awfulness in the scene, as you stand beneath the portals of San Bartolomeo, at whose gayly decorated ceiling you will look for a few moments the next morning, and gaze long and silently upward. Above the lesser tower, the greater appears to loom into the infinitude of blue, its summit lost in night. By day, if day be fair, it will seem to swim and sway in the vault, and you will marvel that beggar and well-to-do citizen do not pass in perpetual dread lest another vast calamity swell the dreadful annals of disaster.

If one dared to quarrel with so charming a portrayer of Italians and Italian scenes as Mr. Howells, it might be in regard to what he says of Bologna. May it not be that he saw the city when the skies frowned, when no ray of sun-light lit any narrow or broad street-arcade, and when, perchance, a dreary rain dripped down? Could Mr. Howells wander into the *"Piazza Vittorio Emanuele"* of a sunny morning, and see the great bronze Neptune and all his mermaids sporting, and see the golden light on the old walls of the two palaces, and the vast pile of San Petronio, I am sure he would have a good word to say for Bologna, in spite of her unattractive arcades ; for, after all, a dull sky and a bad dinner (I remember Mr. Howells has no very high

praise for the *cuisine*,) do color the traveler's impressions in no small degree.

I trust every visitor to Bologna walks
past the Piazza Cavour, with its fresh
and luxuriant bit of greenery, to the
Piazza Galileo. It is a quaint, irregular
space, this latter piazza, where the grass
finds an undisturbed home between many
of the paving stones, and where a statue
of St. Domenico, well-haloed, looks be-
nignly down from a lofty column of
darkened marble. Were I not speaking
of Bologna's streets, I should have more
than one admiring word to say of the
tomb of this good saint that shows so
fairly in a little chapel of the church
here christened for him. It is thought
that Michael Angelo's hand gave some
of the exquisite touches to the all-but-
breathing figures upon the sarcophagus,
and indeed it seems as though some
genius, such as his, must have guided the
chisel that shaped them.

Bologna is a city of pathetic beggars.
They do not swarm, neither do they
come upon you unexpectedly ; but, as
you stray from church to church, and
from palace to piazza, you will ever and

anon descry one shambling toward you
apologetically, quite like a whipped dog
with its tail curved earthward. There
is something sepulchral in the tone in
which they entreat your charity, and I
verily believe each dirty and tattered
suppliant has power, at the effective
moment, to open the flood-gates of the
eyes just far enough to allow one pity-
exciting tear to flow.

You pass the building, once occupied
by the university, where Galvani electri-
fied the scientific world; the palace
where King Enzio was long imprisoned,
(he who sang in wild mediæval times so
sweetly that one of Bologna's fairest
daughters heard love in every tuneful
line); the academy where Raphæl's St.
Cecilia looks forever in holy loveliness
heavenward, and where the spirited
canvases of Elizabeth of Bologna tell
of the lofty genius of the young life so
" untimely taken off." I do not doubt
but that you will wander, too, across a
piazza that steams and glares in the
afternoon sun, where not a shutter is
unbarred, and not so much as an or-
phaned cat is to be seen, to the sycamore

shaded *La Montagnola*. Here the blue-
bloused Italian has a peep into a grassy
paradise. May he not come hither at
any hour and have, *gratis*, a great strip
of sward for a napping place, and the
gently-rustling boughs for a roof? May
he not have, too, at the fruit season, the
early-falling sycamore leaves to whisper
into his dreams Margerita's sweetest
words, and laugh to him her softest
laugh?

How pleasant are Bologna's arcades
when the sun beats down scorchingly!
And yet one tires of them, they are so
interminable, so endless in their monotony of drab and gray and terra-cotta.
To the small street-vender they are an
undisguised blessing. Day-long may
he sit beneath them by his meagre stock
of cheap wares, and doze, or drone
lazily out the excellence of his salable
articles. Delightful glimpses of court-
yard the arcades sometimes afford ; now
a fountain tossing within, the " unsub-
stantial silver of its spray " and now a
fresco to which distance lends an unmis-
takable enchantment.

The Via Roma, that points like an

index finger toward the eternal city, is a pleasant way still, as it was, I am persuaded, in the olden time, and it will lead you, if you follow it to one of the city's many gates, to a promenade and drive much frequented by fashionable Bologna. From the promenade, which is shaded by horse-chestnut trees, across the intervening moat left for many a year to the " annulling surge " of the grass, a fine view may be had of the time-assaulted wall that engirds the city. Further on lie the public gardens, kept with care, and beyond, upon a commanding height, is the pilgrim church of *La Madonna di San Luca*. This looks down upon Bologna as the *Superga* looks down upon Po-laved Turin, and as Fiesole upon Arno-severed Florence.

There is little of the rush and eager press of life in Bologna's streets. Their pulses seldom beat save in measured time. The gayly-dressed officer swings slowly by with his sword and his long cigar ; the bare-headed, dark-eyed women plod along as if they felt something of the burden of the city's age ; the merchants show no insatiable appetite

for trade ; and even the red-guide-
booked traveler loses a little of his **im-**
petuosity when he finds himself winding through highways, where invisible
spirit pedestrians alone companion **him.**

X.

A Walk to Fiesole.

140

X.

A WALK TO FIESOLE.

WHEN it really begins to rain in Italy the downpour seems never-ceasing ; at least, so we thought, as morning after morning we looked up at the narrow strip of sky the Via Pandolfini in Florence allows the dwellers within its precincts to behold. Finally, just as we were in danger of regarding that so common expression, "the blue Italian sky," as a sad bit of irony, day dawned without so much as a wisp of cloud over any peak of the Apennines, and with my friend, the indefatigable Sight-seer, I set forth for Fiesole.

For many a day there had been no allurement in the heights from which this sleepy old town smiles upon the valley, but on this particular morning they were fascinating beyond descrip-

tion. As soon as we had passed the
Piazza Cavour, and had threaded a wide,
winding avenue of sycamores, along
which a steam tramway is laid, Fiesole
stood out clear above us and beckoned
us on. We could scarcely take our eyes
from its cathedral tower, and from the
cypress-girt monastery which stands
upon the spot where, according to tradition, the acropolis of the ancient Roman town once stood. We gave little
heed to the lovely villa gardens, into
which here and there we might have
peered, or to the vineyards where the
grapes hung dusty-purple from vines
that festooned the mulberry trees, and
the figs were bursting over-ripe.

How pure the air was after the rain !
Every breathing creature abroad seemed
to enjoy it. The peasants, women with
baskets, and men driving laden donkeys,
had an unusually animated mien, as if
the clearing of the atmosphere had
swept away a part of the cobweb-tangle
of care from their brains. Only the
oxen moved with the same unvarying,
leisurely stride, and gazed with the
same dreamy look out of their great eyes.

Having restrained my friend, the Sight-seer, from entering the very ordinary bare-façaded church in the little hamlet at the foot of the long, steep ascent, leading directly to Fiesole, we struck into a narrow zigzag roadway, where, until we had mounted some distance, the high garden-walls of villas shut out all view. But as we ascended, these walls ceased to bar our vision, and gradually, wider and wider, the plain of the Arno was outspread before us, with Florence gemming it like a bright cluster of jewels, and the river like a curved sword of tawny gold cutting it in twain. A line of cypress trees, straight, sombre and funereal, appeared to be marching in single file along the roadway far above, so regularly were they planted. These Italian cypress trees are gloomy and mournful when turned into harps by the wind, but they are picturesque and stately when silhouetted against the sky.

When we reached Fiesole, and walked into the piazza where the cathedral stands, just upon the brow of the hill, silence held an unrivaled sovereignty.

There was not a beggar to be seen ; two cab drivers were dozing in their open vehicles under the breezy shade ; two or three merchants were standing in their shop door-ways, lazily smoking the long black cigars of the country ; and the seemingly sole waiter at a small café was tilted back in a rickety chair, gaping vaguely at the heavens. The only person moving was an extremely fat woman, who was waddling across the piazza with a huge basket of vegetables upon her head. The effect of our advent was magical. The two cab-drivers suddenly became very wide-awake, and wished to take us back to Florence at once, although it was evident to them we had just come from there ; the waiter gained his feet with startling alacrity, and assured us that Fiesole wine was very excellent ; the lame, the deaf, the maimed, the blind, came down upon us (minus the purple trappings) as I always imagined, from Byron's poem, the Assyrians must have come down ; and, too, there came from every corner of the piazza bare-headed women and girls with straw-work for sale.

Evidently we were the first objects of prey the horde had that morning, and in fact for some days, beheld, owing to the inclement weather. We were urged, besought and finally commanded to, purchase and bestow, and when, largely on account of the unparalleled effrontery of the creatures, we remained stony-hearted and offered them not so much as the smallest coin, we were regarded with looks of a most menacing character and called names that were not at all pleasant to hear. Had we been without the two stout walking-sticks we carried we should hardly have enjoyed a comfortable feeling of perfect security.

Our triumph over beggars and straw-women in this instance by no means freed us from further persecution. We were besieged at every turn : at the cathedral door where three most hideous, haggard, blear-eyed cripples were sitting; near the entrance to the museum, which is almost barren of interest ; all along the way which leads to the highest point of the town, where the monastery stands. It is stated that some beggars go daily from Florence to Fiesole, which is to them a sort of paradise ; and it is a well-known fact, that not only here, but throughout Italy, the mendicants make themselves look wretched, and even maim themselves, in order to excite sympathy.

We found the cathedral cold, dim and bare, the streets narrow and dirty and the houses for the most part quite as dirty as the streets. But one expects to find very little in Fiesole itself, aside from the remains of the Roman theater ; it is the view to be obtained from the open space just below and in front of the monastery that is the reward for the pilgrimage to this beggar-ridden town. At the foot of a long flight of steps that leads to the entrance of the monastery, stands a stone bench that has the air of being very old, however new it may be. Here one may sit and look and never tire, unless the eye succumbs to the brilliancy of the light. It is true of almost all Italian scenery that a near view of the object or the collection of objects forming a picture, vastly lessens the charm ; it is the distant impression that is grand and beautiful—that is lovely in its uniqueness. Nowhere else are the effects of color the same ; nowhere is there such a perfect blending of hues ; nowhere such lavish richness in the general tone.

Having been driven from the bench of stone by a disagreeable and persistent woman who had small baskets for sale, we ran up the flight of steps toward the monastery. At the summit was a large crucifix,and at its base a skull curiously decorated. We paused here a moment, and looking down received our persecutor's benediction, which was a series of distortions of her not over lovely visage.

We now sought the shelter of a small grove of cypress trees, so cool, so breezy, so full of soft oracular whisperings that had we not realized upon what sacred ground we were standing, we should have been pagan enough to expect to behold a sibyl interpreter. Somehow I feel that the trees themselves would like a return to the former order of things. How much more religious sentiment there is in the thought of a priestess reading through the sweet "lisp of leaves" the secrets of nature

and another world, than there is in the
thought of the sleek, well-fed, lazy
monk, mumbling his prayers and telling
his beads, and having never an eye for
aught beyond the symbols of his faith.

Before turning our backs upon Fiesole,
we paid somewhat grudgingly the ad-
mission fee, and went to look upon the
remains of the Roman theater which lie
upon a slope a short distance back of the
cathedral. Everything was in better
preservation than we had expected to
find it ; the various entrances, the stage,
the tiers of seats and the promenade
have retained, to a remarkable degree,
their original form, when one considers
that for centuries the earth was piled
high above them. Upon our arrival two
cats were occupying two of the choicest
seats, listening perhaps to some spectral
performance. They were evidently not
Roman cats, however, for when the
Sight-seer mounted the rostrum and
began, " Friends, Romans,"—the feline
auditors made a hasty and undignified
exit.

It was pleasant to fall into a long,
rapid stride and go swinging down from

Fiesole. As we drew away from it and looked back, it began to take on again the allurement it had had before we set foot within its piazza. Just as we passed one of the roadside shrines, the interior of which was religiously protected by an iron grating, we rounded a corner and came upon a little old man who took off his hat and wished us good morning. We felt like embracing him and bestowing upon him unnumbered *lire*, for he was the first person who had addressed us, since our departure from Florence, without harboring some sordid motive in his heart. Blessed little old man!

XI.

Seeing Siena.

151

152

XI.

SEEING SIENA.

HAD I a very bitter enemy, I think I might so far forget the admonition " love," as to wish it would sometime be his fate to ride in a compartment of an Italian railway carriage with sixteen others from Montelupo to Empoli, as I once did. We were eight when we reached Montelupo, the limit in first-class compartments. Next me drowsed a handsome young cavalry officer, whose kindly face was not suggestive of combativeness, but whose latent possibilities in that line I discovered when the train halted, and we were invaded by a throng of pleasure-going peasants, who swarmed in upon us with all the bustle of bees. The rudely aroused defender of Italy's liberties pushed his way to the door and shouted to a passing railway official. A

meek, inoffensive, blue-uniformed individual approached, and as he drew near,
a pent-up storm of wrath burst upon
him. In a momentary lull he attempted
to explain matters. Then the six other
gentlemen, who, with the officer and myself had originally occupied the compartment, sprang to their feet and
poured forth a violent torrent of remon-
strance, punctuated with mad gesticula-
tion. Naught did it all avail. The
official shrugged his shoulders and
turned his back upon them.

Another appeared, and the scene, with
some embellishment of language, was
reënacted. It was equally useless. We
were informed we must submit for four
miles—four miles of garlic and odors
unnamed, unless it be in the Montelu-
pian dialect! I fear I failed in politeness
(in the truest sense) to my fellow travelers, in that I did not join in the uproar which they continued to raise. I
preferred to play the part of a spectator
rather than to act in the comedy, for
comedy to me it was, and of the rarest
sort. Finally, the young officer cast
himself into his seat, addressing, as he

did so, a succession of the saints in terms not mentioned in the calendar. The other gentlemen followed with fervor his example. At last the train stopped at Empoli. I hastened to the door, and thus began my journey to Siena.

I wonder if the spirit of the genial Giovanni Boccacio, whose bones repose at his birth-place, Certaldo, that looks down upon Elsa's vale, not many miles away, wandering from some remote sphere to gaze again upon the vine-clad Tuscan slopes, heard all this wordy tumult? If so, he must have thought mankind much the same as they were in those stormy mediæval times he knew.

As you approach, Siena frowns upon you. Indeed, you do not quite recover from the effect produced by her portentous walls and battlements until you enter her quaint precincts, and read upon the arch of the great gate, " Siena opens her heart to you." From that time you and she are in perfect sympathy.

A winding highway leads from the railway station and opens into the Via Cavour, a thoroughfare beautifully paved with large smooth blocks of stone, for there are no sidewalks in Siena ; there would be no room for them. The city is not set upon one hill, but upon several, and the streets are without exception eccentric. They seem to wander up and down at their own sweet will. Sometimes they turn suddenly, sometimes they stop abruptly, but they never pursue any direct course, and they are full of surprises. Now you behold about you nothing but towering walls ; a corner is rounded, and before you are outspread mountain, hill and vale, billowing to the horizon.

It was with much amusement that I had listened the evening previous to a Florentine, who, in his delightful broken English, attempted to describe Siena's streets. " Always they go so," he said, elevating his hands and eyebrows, " or so," dropping both hands and brows. Then, evidently deeming that I had not been sufficiently impressed, he thrice repeated the suggestive pantomime.

I had not been long in Siena when it was my good fortune to fall in with a gracious little gentleman, who, if fine manners be taken as a criterion, could not have been less than a count. My count, then, I shall call him, since he did not see fit to confide to me his name or station, and I felt a hesitancy which I could not overcome, about inquiring into his worldly affairs. In company with Signor Conte 1 went to the cathedral and to the church which is under it. Does it not seem odd to speak of a church as being " under " another ? Yet this is but one of the many strange things you may behold in Siena.

He who would rightly describe the noble cathedral must tell of its wide façade, of its stately campanile that rivals Giotto's Tower, of its marvelous mo-. saics wherein are pictured many a Bible story, of its paintings, its frescoes, its statues, its bas-reliefs. But then he will not have told of the grandeur of its aisles, nor how from above column and arch look down the Popes in long array of gilt and marble. Nor will he have told how the light slants in through the glass of antique windows, of the soft and subdued shadows of the transept, of the grand, the uplifting effect of the whole. Here is a poem written down in the black and white of marble with no unbroken line ; a mighty ode, a symphony that soars eternally to the stars. May it be yours, traveler, to enter these portals some dying autumn afternoon, and, standing before the high altar alone, to hear outside the battling thunder roll.   Pillar by pillar, arch by arch, will the aisles grow into one vast shade-vaulted space, until spirits of another world than ours will seem to people the dim air, and the storm-rent silence to vibrate with the stirring of unseen wings.   Simply a fancy this, to be sure, yet Siena cathedral stirs not only the imagination, but all the deepest emotions of the soul.

That the Piazza del Campo is one of the most imposing squares in the world, no one who has seen it will dream of gainsaying.   Shaped like an amphitheater, sloping toward that splendid structure, the Palazzo Publico, with its majestic bell - surmounted tower, looked down upon by the huge palaces of the ancient nobility, this wide spot was the scene of many a merry festival in the thriving republican days.   Now the grass-blades are the only carnival-makers ; the bubbling fountain mourns ; no plumed cavaliers go swinging by; and the glory of the piazza, with that of all Siena, is a memory of the past.

It was pathetic to note the pride with which my count pointed out to me the grandeur of palace, of church and of square. In him I saw one who seemed to have been born in alien time. I could imagine him flitting about in a gay throng, bowing with stately grace, and bestowing compliments and smiles in his inimitable way. Instead, what a fate was his—to be showing a roving stranger the departed glory of the cherished city of his birth, and giving the same bow and smile to him in return for a few *lire* that of yore would have been given to some fair daughter of a famous house! Farewell, Signor Conte! May kinder fortune be yours in the next world, for I fear you have not many years more to spend in this!

There is in Siena the pensive beauty of desolation and decay. All her greatness has departed from her ; her younger sons have fled to brighter surroundings from the quiet of her sinuous streets ; life is very peaceful within her walls, very unlike that which is stirring in so many cities of new Italy. She still clings to the old, easy, languid ways. Up and down the beautiful, white, long-horned Italian oxen go, blood of that same breed that was sacrificed upon Roman altars ages ago ; back and forth plod the black-stoled brethren of the Misericordia on their errands of mercy ; lazily the peasants prune the vines and pluck the fruit ; and so, wrapped in dreams of days that are no more, serene and fair and sad, sits Siena upon her Tuscan hills.

XII.

A Trip to Tivoli.

XII.

A TRIP TO TIVOLI.

I WENT to Tivoli with Petronio
Brenti. In him the young Roman of the
present time is typified. Dark-eyed,
slender, active, with a politeness that has
a touch of ceremony, he is alive to the
interests of new Italy, and is imbued ·

163

with a belief in the future greatness of
Rome. The city is his ruling passion.
He will tell you that there have been
three epochs of greatness in its history :
the Rome of the Cæsars, the Rome of
the middle ages, and the Rome of to-day
and the future. He will point out to
you with pride the progressive strides
that are being made in every direction,
until you catch his enthusiastic spirit
and glory in the fact that this most
wonderful of all cities is indeed rising
with renewed splendor from centuries of
ruin and decay.

I could but wish that morning that
some of the energy so dominant within
the walls of Rome, might be transferred
to the folk in charge of the railway that
winds toward Tivoli. To be sure I had
a most entertaining companion, who was
very particular to point out to me any objects of interest we passed in crossing the
Campagna ; the views to be had of the
distant snow-capped Sabine mountains
were varied and fascinating, but nevertheless the easy, lazy jog of the train
was exasperating. There was that in
the air which made one desire to partici-

pate in some restless, alert motion—an elixir of life the "stoggy" locomotive did not seem to inhale.

Not very long after the arches of the Claudian Aqueduct ceased to frame vistas of green and gray, we approached the sulphur baths of Aque Albule, where the fashionable Roman bathed in the long ago, and to which the modern Roman is again resorting. Knowing the fondness that the Roman fathers, and likewise their children, had for bath-taking, and the sums of money expended by the State in building and beautifying places where all might indulge in that daily luxury, one can but hail applaus-ively any slight inclination on the part of the living Italian to return to this custom of his dead progenitors.

After many twists and turns of ascend-ing grade we reached Tivoli. We had a glimpse of the falls before we alighted at the station and crossed the Anio to gain the town. It was a holiday, and the streets were thronged. The men were strolling about smoking long cigars, or were gathered in groups upon the corners. The women were gossiping in

front of the small shops, or before
the doorways of dark, uninviting dwellings. A number had assembled about
a well in the largest piazza and were
resting their shapely copper water-jars
upon the ground. We passed some
with these narrow-necked vessels poised
upon their heads. They walked firmly,
with a most graceful carriage, and were
all unconsciously artistic. Some one
has ventured to assert that an Italian
could not be other than picturesque if
he tried. Even the peasants, come from
the far-away vineyards, who went by
with the week's supply of bread—a dozen
loaves perhaps—strung upon a stout
cord and flung over their shoulders, were
grotesquely faultless in pose and movement.

Tivoli stands upon a mountain spur,
and the Villa d' Este, formerly owned
by the famous family of that name, who
ruled so long in princely splendor over
Ferrara, occupies a spot of commanding
beauty. The villa itself has fallen sadly
away from its renaissance magnificence,
but its garden terraces are bowers in
which to dream. From the loftiest ter-

167

race the eye takes in at one sweep a wonderful range. A gray line that sinks into the sky marks the Mediterranean. St. Peter's shows the far-away luster of its dome. Castellated towns crest many lower eminences of the Sabine range. Just where the land ceases to slope, once, amid the cypress trees, nestled Hadrian's villa that was the marvel of many lands, and even now holds the imagination with the charm of crowding memories. Was it not here that the young Antinous, going from shrine to shrine of the pagan gods, discovered the deceit of the priests and the pretended oracles, and bred in his heart that longing for truth and that doubt which led in the after time to his mournful end in the dark waters of the Nile? There are olive orchards on every hand, and vineyards where the famous grapes of Tivoli are grown. To look down upon one of these vineyards is like gazing upon a flat surface of green earth, so thickly do the vines and leaves interlace. Much of the country about Tivoli is a vast flat-topped grape-arbor. But from all the outspread panorama the eye invariably will revert to the villa garden, with its terraces, its long shady paths, its grottoes, its fountains. It is like a bower stolen from fairy land, or a corner of Eden restored to man.

I found lunch at the Hotel Sibylla, with Petronio Brenti, a most enjoyable repast. My companion's sprightliness brightened the dingy interior of the somewhat primitive inn. Signora's broad face became still broader at his greeting, and the sole waiter made so much haste that he all but upset two gouty tables in his eagerness to be expeditious. It gave me an appetite to see the young Roman eat. After the French fashion of breakfasting (which is also the Italian), he had taken only a cup of black coffee and a roll before leaving Rome, so I could hardly wonder that he was as ravenous as a shipwrecked sailor.

But a few steps from the hotel, upon a rocky eminence overlooking one of the falls, stand the temples of Vesta and the Sibyl. How old these temples are can only be conjectured, but it is asserted that they antedate Roman greatness by centuries. One forgets that the great falls of Tivoli are artificial as one watches the whirling mass of yellow water plunge down the rocky abyss. It was indeed a worthy work on the part of Pope Gregory XVI., the tunneling through solid rock and diverting the water of the rushing Anio so that the town should be saved from future inundation. One may look down the gallery through which the main body of water is conducted, and follow it until it leaps madly into the air. And one may, by pathways through luxuriant shrubbery, explore below misty nooks and grottoes, and crossing upon a natural bridge, ascend to where the temples regard the falls with the heavy stoicism of unnumbered years.

Mæcenas had a villa at Tivoli, and, if tradition does not err in regard to its site, an iron manufactory raises its unfriendly bulk upon the identical spot to-day. Who will deny, seeing Italy, the very home of romance, thus invaded, that ours is the Iron Age? What would the noble Mæcenas and his good friend, the poet Horace, say, should they return to earth, gazing where beauty and calm held amicable sovereignty, where fountains plashed in their marble basins

and birds sang in the olive trees, behold
this uncouth monster lifting its grimy
walls?

On Sabine slopes the generous vine
Still yields its store,
And silvery green the olives shine
On Anio's shore.

Still walls and tapering towers you see
The gray hills climb;
But ah! 'tis not the Tivoli
Of olden time.

'Twas beauteous Tibur then; and then
The Sibyl's arm
Held over happy height and glen
A shielding charm.

No harrowing din, no clamor rude,
Might there invade;
But all was soothing quietude,
And sylvan shade.

In dreams the long years backward pass
To those glad days,
And round his villa Mæcenas
With Horace strays.

XIII.

Ascending Vesuvius.

XIII.

ASCENDING VESUVIUS.

THE impudence of the Neapolitan cabman is both exasperating and refreshing. Let the traveler venture forth in the city of the jewel bay, and before he has walked many yards he will either see or hear a cab approaching. He will be addressed, if he has the bearing of an Anglo-Saxon, in some few words of tolerably well-spoken English, joined by sentences of smooth Italian. He will hear of the places he can visit in a few hours if he will but seat himself in the comfortable vehicle ; he will be assured that the horse is a fine animal ; and finally he will be told that his interlocutor is an admirable guide.   This chord will be played upon with variations for a few blocks, and when one driver has ceased another will unfailingly appear to take up the same strain.

To avoid all misunderstanding, haggling and delay, we bargained for our Vesuvian conveyance the night before our intended excursion, and at 9 o'clock upon a breezy, half-clouded autumn morning we took our places in a two-seated open carriage which we found awaiting us at the door.   Our driver greeted us with a nod and a grin, and he continued to smile his approval upon us from his eyes after the laugh had quite disappeared from the lower part of his face.   He had a pleasant, dark eye, · slightly dimmed by age.   His black hair was much streaked with gray, but all his movements were those of a young man.   We liked him from the very first snap of his dexterous whip.

The highway to Vesuvius leaves the Pompeii road at Resina. As we passed out through the suburbs of Naples and the villages of San Giovanni and Portici we met many city-faring folk on foot and in various conveyances. There was the man of business with his carriage and coachman, driving in from his villa; ladies, fashionably dressed, out for a morning's shopping; vegetable and fruit venders with their carts; swarthy workmen guiding huge drays; peasants with heavily-burdened donkeys; and an endless stream of pedestrians, smartly-dressed soldiers, loitering beggars, chattering clerks. A ceaseless babble of talk greeted our ears, and sharp gusts of warm wind blew the fine dust into our faces. At San Giovanni our driver halted and purchased a small bundle of hay; at Portici he procured some meal; at Resina his investment was a long roll of white bread; and ere we left the outskirts of this latter town, he added to his accumulated stores by receiving from the hand of a comely woman, who rushed from a dirty cottage to greet him, a large basket filled with a kind of long sweet red pepper. This was for Bettina who kept a restaurant part way up the mountain. Selecting the largest pepper visible, Jehu took a generous bite and very shortly pepper and a goodly portion of the bread had disappeared.

It was delightful to leave the dirty streets and swarms of ragged children behind, and climb slowly up through vineyards where the grapes were yet ungathered. How tempting the fruit was! Great purple and white clusters bending the festooned vines, whose leaves were beginning to show the first faint tinges of autumn's gold. There were pears that would have dropped into the hand at the lightest touch, and pomegranates ready to yield up the crimson of their hearts. Nor was this all. Figs there were, and apples, too, and olives everywhere ; and there glooming above, was the bulk of the ominous black mountain. At length we came to a lava stream that had buried half a vineyard, and finally the road wound up over vast beds of the molten rock, and only hardy vegetation flourished in spots that had escaped the fiery deluge.

Vesuvius had now the seeming of a terrible evil power. The lava had taken hideous forms : stretched about us there appeared to be vast fields of charred and blackened gigantic human limbs that had writhed into one distorted mass. The scene was like a frightful illusion; and yet to dispel it one had but to turn and cast a backward glance. Below lay the shimmering green of fruit-ful slopes and the dark blue bosom of the bay and the tranquil sea ; Naples upon one side, and beyond the promon-tory of Posilipo, Ischia enwrapt in amethyst haze; Castellamare and Sor-rento upon the other, and Capri's bold heights clear against the western sky.

Presently a guide dashed past us on horseback, and a fellow on foot ran along-side for some distance, volunteering a variety of information. Our northern coldness and indifference finally had a freezing effect upon him and turned him into a statue by the roadside ; so we left him gazing ruefully after us. For more than an hour we had seen the station at the foot of the cone from which the car of the funicular railway takes its de-

parture. As we drew near this point
the atmosphere grew damp and chilly.
From the stable where our driver halted
we raced up a steep footpath to a primitive refreshment room. In half an hour,
it was announced to us, we should pro-
ceed upon our journey. The time
elapsed. We had lunched and were on
hand, but minute by minute passed,
and no one appeared. We stamped
about the station to keep warm. We
wished for a miniature volcano that we
might put it into use as a foot-stove.
We looked in despair upward to see if
there were not some signs of a break in
the cloud that had settled about the
summit ; but no, it grew, seemingly out
of sheer perversity, darker and denser.
Then came the word that all was in
readiness, and we seated ourselves with
a shiver in the open car. Gradually we
moved from the station, and the ascent
began. Just before reaching the upper
station we seemed to rise for a moment
vertically, and there to hang suspended
in air more than a thousand feet above
the place of departure.

On arriving at the terminus of the

railway, a guide was instantly assigned
us, and we started at a swinging pace up
the winding path leading to the crater,
followed by half a-dozen hangers-on,
who offered to carry us in chairs, to pull
us along by ropes and to aid us by push-
ing, and who were much disgusted
because we would have none of them.
Our way led through loose ashes and
fine stones, into which the foot sank to
the depth of two or three inches at
every step. Keeping close together, lest
one should be lost in the dense cloud,
we soon crossed the lava ejected but a
few months previous, struck into a dog-
trot, plunged down a jagged depression,
scrambled upward through smoke and
mist, and stood upon the crater's edge.
We appeared like specters to one another—wraiths magnified in dimensions
by the enveloping shroud. A white,
frost-like moisture covered our faces and
clothing. Some one laughed, and the
sound was hollow and unearthly. We
accompanied our guide along the path
about two feet from the verge of the
crater, and suddenly found ourselves in
the midst of stifling sulphur fumes.

This proved to be the route for descending into the yawning pit.

" Hold on ! " shouted one, whom we had come to call " the Vesuvian enthusiast," from his daily absurd admiration of the mountain ; " I've had enough of this," and he gave a gulp and a gasp. Enough of it we all had had, and a retreat was ordered   I am sure no army put to the wildest rout could have fled in more disorderly fashion than we did from the crater of that volcano. With our guide a yard in advance we went downward in long, flying leaps. Had an eruption been imminent we could not have been more precipitate in our flight. Ashes and stones came in a rattling shower behind us ; the hangers-on, with their ropes and poles, kept panting pace with us, and thus, out of breath, covered with dust and fine particles of rain, we arrived at the railway station. Now, there was no delay. We sprang upon the car, the signal for starting was given, and slowly we left the land of smoke and cloud. What a relief it was to behold once more the vineyards and the sea and the haunts of men! How glad

we were to step from the car, to bid
adieu to that crazy railway, and to go
whirling down the mountain side away
from the gloom, from the black, over-
hanging cone, from the unsightly mass
of the lava beds! Resina, dirty Resina,
was a joy to us after it all, and Naples
was a veritable paradise.

XIV.

La Cava and Paestum.

XIV.

LA CAVA AND PAESTUM.

WE had been at Pompeii the greater part of the day, but there were still some bright hours remaining when we left behind our bronzed and grizzled guide and walked forth from the gate of the silent city. The custodian, unlike that brave Roman of yore who stood true to his post on the night of the town's dark doom, had deserted his place of trust, and was enjoying a peaceful afternoon nap in the shade of a substantial little cabin. We emerged from the dwarfed trees and looked down the roadway, white with dazzling dust. Instantly we were surrounded by boys who desired us to hire their donkeys for the ascent of Vesuvius. In front of the Hotel Diomed we paused and took counsel.

187

It is not a tempting inn, this hotel with
the grand name, and the more we regarded it the less favor did it find in our
eyes.   Then it was that a happy tongue
let slip " La Cava."   The sound was
suggestive of romance.   We hesitated
no longer, but having laid hasty hands
upon our belongings, filed stationward,
escorted by the donkey-boys.   In due
time the locomotive wheezed in, and we
crawled away from Pompeii.

Upon reaching La Cava pride had a
fall.   The sky had clouded and threatened a severe shower, so that we were
forced to take a carriage to the hotel instead of exploring and finding it for ourselves.   Such a vehicle as we tumbled
into, and such horses as dragged us away
from the station !   The steed of Don
Quixote must have been rotund compared with them ; and as for the carriage,
rents let in the four winds of heaven, and
the cushions looked as if within them
there might lie ambushed an army of
creeping, unnamable foes.   However
our driver drew up in front of the Hotel
de Londres, with an explosive flourish of
his whip, and " mine host " received us

as smilingly as if we had arrived with a coach and four.

What a pleasant *Albergo* is the Hotel de Londres! Situated just outside the town, it is bowered in the green of an orchard garden. There is a great roomy hallway into which you walk from the outer air without mounting a single step. Here are arranged plants of lux-uriant growth, and here, too, upon a little desk is the guest-book in which travelers of almost every nationality have not only written their names, but also glowing words in praise of " mine host " and his comfortable roof. Formal prose has not sufficed for some who fancied themselves bards in flower (or at least in the bud), and strewn through the pages of the guest-book are gems of poesy of rare luster!

We had not been in the hotel five min-utes when our good landlord presented us with some bunches of huge purple grapes that were honey to the eye and to the palate. Devouring these, we walked down the sycamore-lined high-road away from the town. The storm that had threatened passed without breaking, and the clouds that scudded swiftly above the mountainous hills were crimsoned with the fading afternoon light. So lofty are the heights surrounding **La Cava** that we lost sight of the sun long ere the dwellers upon the plains we had crossed before plunging into this remote region.

In deep La Cava's vine-girt dale,
* At daytime's close, I saw*
Behind the hills the sunset pale,
* And timorous twilight draw,*
With gentle hand, a vapory veil
* O'er skies devoid of flaw.*

It was so subtile, fine and thin,
* It did not hide a star;*
Day was as though it had not been,
* And noise withdrew afar.*
To darkness felt I close akin,
* And 'twixt us stretched no bar.*

Then for a space I seemed to be—
* Such magic spelled the scene—*
Not in the heart of Italy,
* That sunny-fair demesne,*
But in the home so dear to me,
* Where Kirkland hills are green.*

The sycamore avenue came to an end, and passing a long, low house we saw

through an open doorway a boy practic-
ing upon a flute. He presented a strange
and striking picture. The room in
which he was sitting was so dark that
we could see but a short distance beyond
the door. The floor was littered with
lumps of coal and fagots, and there appeared to be a heap of fire-wood in the
background. Perched upon a stool in
the midst of all this sat the boy, forget-
ful of everything but the tattered sheet
of music which he had leaned against the
broken back of the chair before him.
His black, curly hair fell in tangles
about a cameo-like face ; his gritty fingers
played dexterously up and down the
stops ; he was a mass of rags, but the
very soul of music throbbed within him.

The inhabitants of La Cava seem to
revel in dirt and darkness. The long
main street of the town is lined with
arcades, and from these open dingy, un-
cleanly little shops. Upon poles attached
horizontally in some of the shops, and
without, across the arcades, hung macaroni in surprising variety of form. Huge
two-wheeled carts drawn by two horses
hitched tandem, and crowded beyond

all reason, whirled by with infinite clatter. Knots of brigand-like peasants were gathered here and there. Everything had the air of extreme, but nevertheless picturesque, disorder.

It was very home-like and cheery at the Hotel de Londres that evening. Light fingers ran over the keys of a piano that was really in tune ; there was a ripple of sweet song ; smiling folk strolled about the broad hallway, volubly chatting, and nothing was *out* of tune with the exception of a certain American whom I was ashamed to own as a fellow countryman. This instrument was in perpetual discord and could sound no strain harmoniously. It had evidently been poorly seasoned.

With regret we wrote our names in the guest-book and took our departure the next morning. Moving southward, we came down upon Salerno with its orange groves and its span of sapphire gulf, and then were off again through a level vineyard country. After a time we left the vineyards behind and traversed desolate, undulating pasture land that billowed away to the sea. Here herds of

strange looking brown cattle were grazing, and here it was that the desperate
brigand Manzi was wont, near the rushing river Sele, not many years agone, to
swoop down upon the venturesome traveler. The government had disposed of
Sir Brigand, but Malaria remains unvan-
quished. We caught occasional glimpses
of high-booted, large-hatted herdsmen,
sometimes on foot and sometimes
mounted upon small ponies ; save for
their presence the country was almost
tenantless.

With the city Paestum, time and van-
dal hands have made sorry havoc, but
with her grand temples, as though in
reverence, they have dealt generously.
There are traces, in the shape of grass
and shrub-o'ergrown mounds, of the
walls that once inclosed the sturdy,
Greek colonial town, and one lonely,
crumbly gate-way still stands in defiance
of the fate that has overtaken the others.
A single genial-faced railway official
reigned over the neat station where the
train left us. He bustled about as if
desirous of doing us some service, but
as a straight highway in full view led

toward the dead city's unguarded gate; we could not take advantage of his evident kindliness, so wished him a good morning and hurried on. The day was wonderfully clear, and a soft breeze was stirring. Behind us, in the far background, their grayish white slopes glowing in the sunlight, lay the Apennines. Before us the narrow, little-traveled roadway skirted a high plaster-covered wall which enclosed an orchard and the only house of any size standing within the confines of what *was* Paestum. This wall entirely shut out our view upon one side, and not until we came to a highway at right angles with the one we were following, did the majestic Temple of Neptune and the Basilica meet our vision. Alone in the midst of a wide uncultivated field they stand, where briars and vines and rank grass hold riot. The temple, far grander than the hall of justice, wears lightly its two thousand years. Fluted column and carven capital, in stately line upon line, uphold the massive cornice. You climb the few great steps and enter the temple's portals. How vocal the silence is! What

195

strange stories of eld might every column
tell, of festival, of sacrifice, of war!
Seen between the pillars as through a
vista, beyond the intervening meadow
and marish land, dances and foams and
shimmers the blue bosom of the Mediterranean.   Nowhere in all Italy (unless
it be within the Colosseum) is one impressed with the glory and the vastness
of the past as one is here.   The present
becomes a dream, the past is the reality.
Even the lizard, dozing in the sun and
rustling away through the weeds at your
approach, is a part of the long ago.   Is
it not akin to the one some lithe young
Greek girl watched above her on the
bough as she sat beneath a laurel's
woven shade in a well-walled garden-
close, where a fountain plashed in its
marble basin and a hidden brown bird
twittered plaintively?

Ere we again passed beneath the
crumbling city gateway, we visited the
Basilica and the Temple of Ceres; but
the Temple of Neptune remained the
shrine of our worship.   I shall always
love to take memory for a guide, and
roam where priestly sandals once trod,

seeing with no uncertain vision the sapphire sea, the ambered slopes of the Apennines and those symmetrical columns that have heard the pulse-beat of twenty centuries.

XV.

Over the Tête Noire.

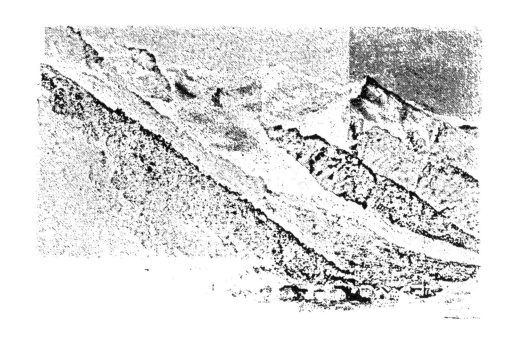

XV.

OVER THE TÊTE NOIRE.

SHOULD good fortune land you safely
in Martigny some clear and cool Sep-
tember evening, that same happy genius
will undoubtedly lead your footsteps to
Hotel Clerc. There will the proprietor
welcome you with a suave and smiling
bow; there will the bland head-waiter
greet you in the very bad English that
flows so glibly from the tongue of many
a foreign chief functionary; and there
you will be shown to a scrupulously
clean, uncarpeted apartment, whose

201

windows will invite you to linger long
in contemplation of the moon-lit valley
of the Rhone.   Table d'hôte will be announced when you descend to the hotel
office, and, after eating your way through
six or seven leisurely courses, the night
will beguile you to wander forth beneath
its star-sown dome.   Through your
dreams may float visions of an ancient
fortress tower, as picturesque as the
celebrated mouse-tower of the Rhine ;
for down upon Martigny, from its pin-
nacle of rock, looks a gray, embattled
fragment of a castle that has seen the
centuries glide by since the days of
doughty knight and tournament.

You will thrill with delight if blue sky
gleams above you when you glance
heavenward the next morning, after
having been roused at six by no very
gentle tap upon your door.   If there
chance to be a thin mist, or a few white
clouds hovering about the higher peaks,
there will arise in your breast a faith
that the sun will disperse them, and you
will hurry down to the hot coffee and
rolls and honey awaiting you below.
Where the bees pilfer the subtle, not-to-

be-analyzed sweetness that pervades the liquid amber, let some epicure decide. When the heathen deities reigned on Olympus, Jove must have sweetened his nectar and his temper with it.

Jehu awaits you at the door with two sturdy steeds. Up you spring. Proprietor, head-waiter, porter, and various supernumeraries, wave their adieux, the latter with smiles indicative of the size of the fees you have bestowed. You are whisked around a corner, and Hotel Clerc becomes a memory—and a pleasant one.

You wind through the streets of Martigny-Bourg, a quaint, dirty, dingy old hamlet, and soon begin the ascent of the Col de la Forclaz. Jehu points out a white chalêt upon the mountain above. " In three hours we shall be there," he tells you in French. Would you rival Jehu and reach the chalêt more than half an hour sooner? Descend from your seat then where the old mule path leaves the roadway at one of the small hamlets through which you pass, and follow its steep and stony course. You will find yourself at Chevans with leisure

to devour all the grapes the peasant
children offer you before Jehu arrives.

You have left the terraced vineyards
and pear orchards behind. Below and
far away reaches the Rhone Valley, and
the river looks like a silver serpent
outstretched upon a plain of gleaming
emerald. You pass an occasional family
of peasants going valleyward—children,
cow, goat, pig, form the van of these
rustic cavalcades. The head of the
house and his good wife come plodding
patiently on in the rear, laden with many
burdens, just returning from some high
mountain pasturage for the fruit harvest.
At last you emerge from the forest of
pine and fir, and find yourself at the
summit of the Col de la Forclaz. A
rotund peasant, with a rubicund face,
appears at the doorway of the mountain
inn and beamingly bids you enter.
Presently you are summoned by Jehu,
and discover that one horse has been
detached from your chariot and is
meditatively leading the way down the
narrow winding road. For half an
hour you descend slowly to the picturesque valley and village of Trient,

where a somewhat primitive dinner awaits you.

Before you plunge into the dark forest it is high noontide. Near brawls a mountain torrent, above towers the Tête Noire. Slowly you ascend, and then the valley of the Eau Noire, and, nestling upon the opposite declivity, the hamlet of Finhaut, burst upon the view. Again one steed becomes your guide, and now down a narrow roadway cut in the face of the cliff, while hundreds of feet sheer beneath foams and roars the wild, rushing stream, you follow your four-footed leader. Beetling granite bowlders menace darkly. Now you are hidden from the hot eye of day in a roughly-hewn tunnel, where the voice has an unearthly sound ; now you pass the spot where an avalanche overwhelmed some ill-fated travelers ; and now you are at Chatelard—half way.

Ere long, in dazzling whiteness, Mont Blanc and the adjacent peaks dawn upon your vision. You cross from Switzerland into Savoy. The road becomes broader and smoother. Through a châlet-dotted vale you wind until another

long ascent is reached.   At length the
last eminence is climbed, and down you
whirl toward Chamouni.   Clearer gleam
the "needles" of Mont Blanc, but no
nearer seems its dome-like summit.
Soon you are at Argentiers, in the Valley of the Arve.   Before you opens the

"Vale of Chamouni;" at the left lies
the Argentiers Glacier.   The fields
widen ; peasant women are making
hay ; cowbells jangle on the air.   There
is the Mer de Glace—that mighty, sinuous, creeping river of ice—and there is
Montanvers, whither you will one day
climb to look down upon the ice-choked
chasm.

Now, in the mellow light of waning

afternoon, glisten the red roofs and the white walls of Chamouni. Jehu's whip explodes in a series of startling cracks, the horses bound swiftly forward, and down the dusty high-way, past groups of guides, and pedestrians of many nationalities, you dash into the heart of the town.

XVI.

Hertenstein.

XVI.

HERTENSTEIN.

WHAT delightful tricks does the elf Fancy sometimes put upon us! It was but yester afternoon, while sitting by my favorite western window, gazing out upon a deserted, fast-whitening street, that this willful fairy made magical change in the dreary scene.

Suddenly, before me spread a summer landscape. I saw a glassy lake, a cloudless sky, and mountains whose peaks glistened like giant crystals in the sunlight. It all came back to me again—Lucerne, and those wonderful August days at Hertenstein. There stood the Pension Château, rising invitingly near the water's edge, with its shady balconies and its unpicturesque tower. I stepped from the steamer at the landing, and wended my way through shady alleys and by winding paths toward its hospit-

211

able door. Madame smiled upon **me**,
and welcomed **me** in her eccentric English. Her merry little daughters were
tripping about the wide hall-way. The
sound of guttural German and vivacious
French floated in from the outer air. I
greeted   friendly   faces   and   clasped
friendly hands, and wandered out beneath the doming blue again, meeting
the spry Fräulein, whose cheery " Voilà,
Monsieur," greeted me every morning
when she brought in the delicious coffee
and hot milk.

Aromatic breezes blew down from the
looming ridges of the Rigi ; great drops
of dew still beaded the grass on the
southern hillside, where the plums hung
their dusky globes, and where the cheeks
of the pear and apple were crimsoning.
On I went, through paths that the laurel
bowered, to the chestnut wood. Here
was a presage of autumn ; for the russet
leaves came silently floating down, and
far and near were thickly dotting the
mossy sward. The motion of their descent seemed rhythmical ; and there
came to my mind fancies about the
falling of leaves :—

Tiny mariners of air,
Brief the voyage on which you fare,
Drifting down a crystal tide,
By the sunlight glorified.

Soon, while wailing winds sweep by,
Sadly stranded you will lie,
Seeking harbor nevermore,
Wrecked upon an alien shore.

From mound and hollow, slender-stemmed lavender flowers like the crocus were peeping ; and now, in the topmost boughs, the locusts began to rasp upon their discordant viols. Below, in a meadow that bordered a thick grove of pines, two strong-armed, swarthy-browed sons of the land of Tell were swinging monotonous scythes, ever and anon droning an unmelodious folksong. Near by, their toil-wrinkled spouses were pressing the partially dried hay into deep baskets, to be borne away upon shoulders long accustomed to bend under such burdens.

An occasional drowsy bird-note blent with the strident sounds of the cicadas ; and, as I zigzagged down a slope from the chestnut grove to the broad orchard road, hard and smooth, before me rose the wooded promontory where once stood the old Schloss Hertenstein, now but a memory. I pictured its ruined walls, the ivy growing over them, the vacant windows, the crumbling watch-tower.

I passed a weather-beaten barn. The sign above the low doorway appealed to me—"Fresh milk, ten centimes per glass." How delicious it was, and such glasses! Coming upon a rustic chair at a spot that commanded a charming view of the lake, I read on a large stone near at hand this inscription : "Queen Victoria sat in this chair, when she visited Hertenstein." Below was the date. I fear this sent no thrill through my breast. Neither tree nor flower assumed an added beauty, nor did the scene out-spread before me take on a greater charm. I could not share the feeling of the individual who undoubtedly would, a few moments later, with undisguised satisfaction repose in that sacred seat!

Is not that borderland between day and night, called "twilight," beautiful amid the most unromantic surroundings?

What, then, shall I say of it at Herten-stein?

I embarked ere the set of sun in a trim row-boat. The water was ripple-less : there was not a quiver amid the reeds along the shore. Dreamily I pulled the oars, and gained the sapphire bosom of the tranquil lake. Far away, straight in air, rose a thin pillar of smoke from the steamer approaching Vitznau, laden with the Rigi-seeking tourists, going up for the sunrise. The red sun was fast sinking ; and, ere I drifted in the purple shadow of massive Bürgenstock, towering sheer above the symmetrical firs that skirt its base, I caught the last sight of the fiery disc be-hind a shoulder of Pilatus, the monarch of the peaks that sentinel Lucerne. Now what a delicate tint hued water and sky, and enwrapt like a web of gossamer the mountain sides ! Every drop that drip-ped from my oars seemed a liquid ruby, and I was floating upon a tide whose color rivaled the leaf that is nearest the rose's heart.

Pilatus is a grand mountain. Rugged, precipitous, majestic, it symbols both

power and repose. In the morning sun
it is stern, almost threatening ; in the
subdued evening light it is peaceful,
softened, clothed in the garb of dreams.

On one of Pilatus' slopes is a lonely
wood-girt lake, as gloomy and melan-
choly-breathing as the dismal tarn of
Poe's " House of Usher." How strange
are legends ! for hither, we read, Pon-
tius Pilate, when banished from Jerusalem, wandered in wild remorse, and
drowned himself in the dark, somber
waters, and from the exiled Jewish ruler,
the legend says, the mountain received
its name.

Faintly, far away, before the shadows
deepened, could I detect châlets here
and there, with their picturesque gables
and windows, whence erelong beacon
lights would gleam down the purple
hall-ways of the dusk. Slowly, through
the falling shades, I sought Hertenstein
once more. As I stepped to the land,
the night air that swept in gusts along
the darkened, leaf-roofed alleys was red-
olent with the perfume of roses. There
were the cheery lights in the long din-
ing-hall. The lights? Ah ! yes, but

glimmer came from my neighbor's
windows across the way. I was no
longer at Hertenstein, and I turned with
a sigh from
the fast-thick-
ning winter
night and the
flake-filled
air. It had
been but a
vision after all ; yet
who will say that it
was not a pleasant one?

The fields are stoled in white,
The storm-winds shrilly whine,
And memory to-night
Recalls fair Hertenstein ;

Recalls the August days
Of sunlight-flooded sky,
The song bird's mellow lays,
The low wind lapsing by.

Again I wander where,
While dying summer grieves,
Come drifting down the air
The amber chestnut leaves.

Again I seem to float
　　Upon thy breast, Lucerne,
While round my drifting boat
　　The fires of sunset burn.

Once more my eyes behold
　　The charmèd moon rise up,
Pouring its generous gold
　　From out a brimming cup.

How clear each distant scene!
　　The roses all a-blow;
The woodland, darkly green,
　　Where stood the old château;

The winding paths that pass
　　Beneath the whispering boughs;
The orchard's waving grass;
　　The mountains' grizzled brows.

And while the dim hours flee,
　　Till morn makes rosy sign,
Still be my dreams of thee,
　　Of thee, fair Hertenstein!

XVII.

Around Tombstone on Burro-Back.

XVII.

AROUND TOMBSTONE ON BURRO-BACK.

IT was dusk in Southern Arizona. Standing on the platform of Fairbanks Station, I watched, with a feeling akin to loneliness, the receding train that was speeding rapidly toward Mexico. The environment of a railway station is seldom picturesque, and the surroundings of this were no exception. A deserted adobe hut that stood some rods distant, upon the opposite side of the track, encompassed by a dilapidated *corral*, was the sole object that attracted the eye in a dreary waste of rock and sand. Barren foothills rose here and there, as gray as the dense clouds that were massing along the horizon, and above them towered straggling mountain peaks, upon whose summits and sides lay vast patches of

221

snow that seemed to take the form of crosses and gigantic monoliths.

A pair of prancing Mexican ponies bore me away from the civilizing pathway traversed by the locomotive, along one of a dozen trails which penetrated the hills. In the desolation that brooded over all, there was a grandeur which inspired awe. The solemn stillness, devoid of cry of beast or bird, forced one to look and listen, and rendered the gravest comment trivial. Each muffled stroke of the ponies' hoofs upon the sandy soil became intensified in sound. The dry buffalo grass rustled weirdly in the chilly night breeze that stole down from the snow fields; and, as darkness began to draw closer her sable curtains, the stories of the robberies and murders committed in the earlier days of the mining excitement, rose with unpleasant distinctness before the mind's retina.

Up through the rocky gulches for seven miles the tireless little animals dashed, until at last the lights of Tombstone began to twinkle in the distance. They were a cheery and welcome sight.

I would not recommend a timid traveler to attempt the journey by night. Traversing the ground afterward in the prosaic light of day, I had occasion many times to marvel how it was ever safely accomplished in what was almost Egyptian darkness. Scarcely once was the pace slackened, for the ascent, though continuous, was gradual. The light wagon swayed from side to side, scurried through sandy places, leaped as buoyantly as a boy over countless obstructions, and finally deposited me uninjured before the doorway of a hospitable cottage.

My first impressions of Tombstone were vague. Passing rapidly through the wide main street, dotted on either side by brilliantly lighted saloons where gambling was going on in public view, the hurried glances which I cast here and there afforded me but little idea of what I was to see on the morrow. A motley throng was threading the principal thoroughfare ; there was all the noise and gayety of a city, but so suddenly was it left behind that it seemed like an hallucination.

To know Tombstone accurately one must cease to be a "tenderfoot," a transformation which requires time. I fancy I never quite emerged from that state, there regarded as so unfortunate ; nevertheless I succeeded in acquiring, in rather a novel way, some interesting facts in regard to the "city of the whited sepulchre."

One sunny morning, about a week after my arrival, I was seated upon the steps of "Contention Cottage," looking down upon the town, half a mile away. In the extension which was used as a kitchen, Jim, the negro man of all work, and Sam, the Chinese cook, were discussing a shooting affray that had occurred the night before. The great pumps of the mine close at hand were throbbing monotonously, and the sound of rushing water mingled with the oaths of Mexican teamsters, who were loading ore just below an enormous pile of débris, came distinctly to my ears upon the rarified mountain air. These peons habitually swear in English, the only use for which the language is fitted, according to their way of thinking. They are a miserable

set, lazy, filthy, and terrible thieves
withal. I was watching their great wagons, drawn by twelve or fourteen mules,
wind slowly down the hill, when another
object of interest appeared upon the
scene. The new attraction emerged
from behind a gigantic cactus a few rods
distant, and slowly approached the cottage. But that it was smaller, I should

at first have taken the intruder to be an ordinary mule. I called to Jim, who stuck his head from the door, grinned at me, and announced in answer to my inquiry that the animal was a stray burro. His burroship was inclined to be friendly. When at last he paused but a few yards away, he regarded me with a look which seemed to say, " I am at your service." I knew the summary manner in which horse thieves were usually dealt with upon the frontier ; but this did not occur to me until I had procured a halter and captured the burro. Jim, whom (for the want of a better) I accepted as my mentor, quickly quieted my fears by telling me that if I cared enough for the creature to feed it, no one would gainsay my right of possession. So, not without some little pride, I led my prize (for such he afterward proved) down to the stable. My first task was to find a name for my strangely acquired quadruped. As my knowledge of Spanish was unfortunately small, I was obliged to resort to " Don Quixote " for a cognomen, and thus the burro came to be christened Sancho.

That afternoon, having been successful in my search for a saddle, I mounted
Sancho in the stable yard, and found,
much to my delight, that he was accustomed to a rider, and was fairly tract-
able. Before many days had passed, I
so familiarized myself with his tricks and
whims that I ventured forth some miles
along a smooth trail which led to the
south.

In two weeks' time Sancho and I were
the best of friends. I had never ridden
him into town, and not having fully sat-
isfied my curiosity in regard to the ins
and outs of the place, I resolved to make
the pilgrimage on burro-back. I started
without the least trepidation, notwithstanding the ludicrous spectacle which
I doubtless presented. Taking the most
circuitous route, which led past the hoist-
ing works of several mines I had not before visited, I finally reached the head of
Allen Street, which is the Broadway of
Tombstone.

It was a clear, mild day, and long
rows of ox and mule teams were standing in front of the saloons and stores.
Dashing horsemen, " frontier dandies,"

as some call them, with their great top-
boots, jingling spurs, velvet jackets, and
sombreros, corded with gold braid, were
riding ostentatiously about, much to the
disgust of the shaggy-bearded miners
and ranchmen, who regarded them with
the utmost contempt. Among the throng
the " almond-eyed celestial " was often
visible. Nearly every nationality upon
the globe was there represented, such is
the magnetic influence of a rich mining
camp. The buildings, almost without
exception, had " battlement " fronts,
and were of but one story. The dwelling houses were scarcely more preten-
tious. Above the commodious court-
house, the only edifice which deserves
particular mention, the stars and stripes
were floating, for Tombstone is a county
seat. Throughout this region adobe
brick, manufactured in a simple way
from a kind of adhesive soil that is widely
found, is the favorite building material.

A few years ago the place was the
haunt of the rattlesnake, prairie dog,
and coyote. Now it is called a city, and
boasts two daily papers. It sprang into
existence as though through the aid of

the genie of Aladdin's lamp. Two miners who were out prospecting noticed the rocky hills. One suggested to his comrade that they should see what they could find there. " You will find your tombstone if you make the venture," was the reply he received. Thus the place came to be named, for the miner's prophesy did not prove true. Tents and ugly board shanties began to dot the hill-sides. From California, from Nevada, from Mexico, and from the East, men flocked to the new field. In those days there was no Southern Pacific ; the trails led through an uninhabited, treeless, Indian-infested land. The town grew apace, then the flames leveled it, but it was as tenacious of life as the fabled Phœnix, and triumphantly rose from its ashes.

As I turned Sancho's head homeward, and slowly ascended one of the hills, five mountain ranges shortly became visible. Far beyond the Mexican frontier two peaks of the San Jose chain pierced like dark bulwarks the purple distance ; in the north the Santa Catalinas lay in massive proportions along the horizon ; while at other points the

Dragoons, Whetstones and Huachuchas, all snow-capped, notched the sky.

Leaving Sancho to browse among the rocks and cactus, I approached the entrance to the Contention mine. The foreman, who was a genial fellow, chanced to be upon the point of descending, and invited me to accompany him. This mine is the richest of the many that honeycomb the hills surrounding Tombstone. With its drifts, cuts, slopes, and winzes, it has more than twenty miles of tunneling. We took candles and stepped into the cage. The engineer pulled the lever, the great wheel of the lowering apparatus revolved, and we shot swiftly downward into impenetrable darkness. A current of warm air eddied about us as we flashed by level after level. Down, down we were borne— four hundred, five hundred, six hundred feet, and then, like one in a dream, I stepped out of the cage and found myself in a rocky chamber where two candles, stuck in opposite crevices, shed a pale, flickering light. Half a dozen miners, whose dust-laden faces and beards gave them a weird and pallid

look, were waiting to ascend. I watched
them disappear, and, having lighted my
candle, followed the foreman through
the main drift along a neatly laid track,
where we occasionally passed men push-
ing cars laden with ore or valueless rock.

Having proceeded for some distance,
my guide turned into a narrow cut at
right angles to the one we previously
had been traversing. Here, in a deep
winze, two miners were at work upon a
vein of unusual richness.

Contention ore contains both gold
and silver, the former, however, in small
quantities. The amount of timber that
is weekly lowered into the mine, to be
used in supporting the various galleries,
is enormous. So great is the caution
exercised that an accident is of rare occurrence. The vigilant and far-seeing
superintendent, recognizing the rights
of labor as well as capital, has made the
mine a place of success and content,
rather than " contention," as its name
might imply. The air in the drifts is af-
fected but little by atmospheric changes,
and the currents that circulate freely,
owing to the fact that all of the levels

are connected, have an agreeable warmth. The "stoping," or working toward the surface, I found to be the most interesting feature in this style of mining. Tombstone mines are remarkable for their cleanliness, and there is nothing to detract from the pleasure of visiting them. Having viewed the various points of interest, my guide piloted me back to the main shaft ; and, although I had experienced no fear, it was with a feeling of relief that I gazed once more upon the blue sky and golden sunlight. Sancho welcomed my return with a resonant bray—a sound which can be appreciated only by those who have heard it—and frisked with delight when I guided him stableward.

My next excursion on burro-back was more ambitious. Having been invited to visit Contention City, nine miles distant, where the crushing mill of the mine is situated, I chose a cloudless morning, saddled Sancho, and, armed with a rough map containing directions in regard to the course to pursue, set out. The trail is so much traveled by teams dragging the ore-that I had no difficulty in following it. Half a mile out of Tombstone, by the side of the stream flowing from the mining pumps, sat two hideous Mexican women, pounding clothes upon a smooth rock. Their apparel looked as if it needed the same cleansing process, and their hair as though it had never known the subduing influence of comb or brush. Near by were their huts, miserable, low structures of adobe, thatched with coarse grass. I passed one shanty made entirely of tin cans flattened, and nailed upon poles firmly planted in the earth. This was a palace compared with some of the hovels I encountered. The country was entirely barren of vegetation ; low mesquite bushes and numerous varieties of the cactus, however, were abundant. Upon a certain species with long, blade-like leaves, the Apaches are said to impale their captives, and leave them to perish beneath the scorching sun—a refinement of cruelty which even the horrors of the Inquisition never equaled.

About three miles from Tombstone the trail entered a kind of park, where rocks in the most fantastic shapes rose on every hand, or were piled one upon another. It seemed as though the children of giants had used the spot for a play-ground. Further on, the bowlders assumed the form of Titanic monuments, as perfect of outline as though fresh from under the sculptor's chisel. The weird desolation which pervaded this place added in a great measure to the effect produced by these huge masses of stone.

The many gulches threaded by the trail bore traces of the floods which, in summer, when a storm-cloud bursts, sweep through them with boisterous violence. I paused to examine one of great depth, where a famous attempt had been made to rob the stage, which formerly ran regularly from Benson, the nearest point upon the Southern Pacific road, to Tombstone. The highwaymen shot the driver, but the express messenger seized the reins, lashed the horses to their highest speed, and escaped. The thought of the fusillade which for a few moments was kept up between the occupants of the coach and the robbers, made me feel a little creepy, and as Sancho seemed inclined to quicken his pace, I did not insist upon a long tarry. From the summit of a narrow divide I at length descried Contention City, which consists of the mill, the railway station, a deserted hotel, one store, and a number of adobe houses. Far away along the plain I could trace the course of the San Pedro river, by the deep channel worn in the yielding soil. From this stream, by powerful pumps, the water is raised to the summit of the hill, upon the side of which the Contention crushing mill is located. As I entered this building with its superintendent, having previously seen Sancho comfortably cared for, a deafening din greeted my ears. I might have closed my eyes, and easily believed myself to be in Pandemonium. The noise of swirling water mingled with the incessant thud of the stamps, and above all was heard the crunching of the rock-breakers that seized the solid chunks of ore in their voracious jaws, and crushed them like so many walnuts. Over these fragments, which the stamps reduce to powder, rushes a stream of water; quicksilver is

236

introduced to collect the particles of precious metal, which is finally converted into bullion by a heating process, and cast into bars for shipping. It was high noon when I left Contention City, and slowly ascended the divide from which I had obtained my first view of the town and the San Pedro valley. Mexican teamsters, with their ore wagons, were toiling lazily along just ahead, and one was monotonously droning a Spanish air. I had no desire for the companionship of these surly fellows, so, putting Sancho through his best paces, they were speedily left behind.

Not many days afterward, as twilight was falling, I took my last ride on burroback. A ten minutes' climb brought me to the summit of Contention Hill. Arizona is the land of beautiful sunsets, and that night the panorama of color that moved across the heavens seemed like the gorgeous dyes of a tropical dream. From behind the snow-crested Huachuchas the crimson glow reached with constantly varying radiance to the zenith. Between these silver peaks and where the Santa Catalinas uploomed was a spot that shone like a flame of living fire. No wonder that the Spaniards, who saw the mountains in the olden time, thought that beyond them lay the long sought Eldorado.

1884.

XVIII.

Bermudian Vistas.

XVIII.

BERMUDIAN VISTAS.

I.

THE TRIP OUT.

IF one is about starting upon an ocean voyage he naturally hopes that the auspices will be favorable. He watches the sky to see if gathering clouds will not disperse; he marks the weather-

241

vane and calculates upon the chances of
a change of the wind to a fair quarter.
Midwinter skies are not often kindly,
and midwinter winds are obstinately
keen, so the sea-going traveler may
count himself lucky if either be genial.
On a certain midwinter Monday neither
was pleasant to contemplate. A cloud,
dense with sifting mist, hung over New
York, and even the waves of the bay
looked angry. At half-past two in the
afternoon the wharf of the Quebec
Steamship Company presented a lively
appearance, notwithstanding the inclement weather.

In half an hour the steamer Trinidad
would sail for Bermuda. A bevy of
young ladies had come down to see a
friend off, and there were flowers and
kisses in profusion. A young English
officer, going out to the military station
at the islands, looked on with an interested and amused air. Jolly Captain
Fraser made his way about among the
passengers, having a cheery word for
everybody. Good byes were finally cut
short by the deafening noise of the
chief steward's bell, and the sharp toot-

ing of the steamer's whistle. Down
the gangway hastened the shore-going
folk, the plank was raised, the cables
cast off, and the vessel swung slowly out
into mid-stream. From deck and pier
there were cheers and waving of hands
and hats and handkerchiefs. Then the
mist began to enshroud familiar objects. The great span of the Brooklyn
bridge grew indistinct; the caricature
of a fort on Governor's Island was lost
to view ; the guardian Statue of Liberty
became like a specter ; the shores seemed
to sink and melt into the horizon, and
finally even the tower on Coney Island
was but a memory. The melancholy
bell-buoys had sounded their last "ding
dong" in our ears, and we were fairly
at sea, as some of us soon came un-
pleasantly to realize. Anticipation,
however, had been worse than reality
proved to be, and with rugs and wraps
and steamer-chairs life still held its
joys. Some tried mariners promenaded
the deck, while others explored the various nooks and crannies of the ship.

A rowboat had long since put out
from one of the white-sailed harbor

sloops and taken off our pilot, so now there was nothing for idle eyes to watch save the waves, the occasional passing vessels and the scenes on deck. Sailors went and came ; awnings were put up, and many of the preparations for a long ocean voyage appeared to be in progress. None of us felt that in two and a half days we should be in summer land, and heartily glad to have arrived. At dinner that night everybody was jolly. The characteristics of various passengers had already become evident. The *enfant terrible* was among us. He got under every one's feet and pestered the ship's people from the common sailor up to the captain. The nautical crank was present. He knew all about the ship, and was bent on imparting his knowledge to whomsoever he could "button-hole." There was the smart young lady and the dowdy English matron ; and there was the maiden aunt, heaven bless her for her large-hearted soul ! But this is not a catalogue, and yet we must not forget our friend, the professor— the happy, the ever merry.

Some truthful writer has said that to

reach the "Bermudian paradise" you must pass through purgatory, and Mark Twain, one is not surprised to find, puts it even stronger. We had a taste of something about ten o'clock that Monday night which certainly was not paradise. What a frolic the wind had in the rigging, and what a game of toss and catch the waves played with the stanch Trinidad!

"Oh nothing, nothing," the captain said the next morning, with one of his hearty laughs, "just a bit of sea on."

Most of us wished his "bit of sea" had been "on" in other latitudes.

The few who gathered at breakfast tried to "make believe" hungry, but over porridge and the most tempting morsels of beefsteak their faces were not happy. It was a dreary day that followed. Rain, rain, rain; and gusts that blew it everywhere. There was no comfort to be taken on deck, and the unfortunates who were below were too dismal to utter a word. Once the sun showed a watery gleam, but speedily hid behind a cloud as if ashamed of so discreditable a performance.

The hours dragged wearily by. During the afternoon those who were not asleep wished they were, and Bermuda—how far away it seemed !

But Wednesday morning revived drooping spirits. The sun shone with no uncertain glow. Great patches of sea-weed rode by on the crests of the waves. The wind was astern and the huge square sail was set. The report was circulated that we were making splendid time. Some one declared, that the captain had said we should sight St. David's light before ten that evening. Joy was visible on every face. A " running sea " was small matter now. What if the boat did occasionally lurch to starboard until her rail nearly dipped in the waves ! Tied securely into steamer chairs the most timid speedily became brave. We passed a close-reefed schooner at mid-morning which proved to be a very diverting occurrence, so easily is one amused at sea. And what a merry, happy-go-lucky meal dinner was ! To manage a plate of soup and not spill it into the lap of a neighbor required almost the skill of a juggler. Dishes of every description went tobogganing up and down and across table, and there sounded an occasional alarming crash from the pantry. But the stewards were all good natured. Doubtless they were glad to see so many of the passengers in the saloon, and to be relieved from dancing attendance on sundry staterooms.

Toward nine o'clock all was expectancy. At least half of the sky was star-dotted. Every five minutes we rushed out from the general gathering-place at the top of the companionway to scan the horizon. At last, just before ten, our persistency was rewarded. Far, far ahead, upon the right, when we rose on the crest of a wave the fixed star of a lighthouse shone. Shortly afterward the flash-light on Gibb's Hill saluted us with its recurring, brilliant beam, and then we saw the faint glimmer from the barracks on St. George's Island. We did not retire until we lay under lee of the land and had heard from the pilot's own lips that he would come on board early the next morning.

At dawn there was a great bustle on deck—a rattling of cordage, a creaking

of windlasses, and an incesssant tramp-
ing of feet.   Erelong we were under
way.   Before the seven o'clock breakfast
everybody had taken a peep at the land.
We saw low, undulating hills, half
covered with dark cedar trees, and,
dotted on crest and in depression, were
the white Bermudian cottages.   Faces
we had not beheld since the afternoon
of our departure were visible again at
the breakfast table, pale many of them,
but smiling, for were we not about to
put foot on solid earth once more?

Now we were abreast of Ireland Island
and its noted dock and fortifications ;
now we had taken on another pilot,
number one having boarded the ship at
daybreak ; now we were threading a
circuitous channel, past Sheep Island,
and Marshall Island, and Godet Island,
and now we were in Hamilton harbor.
There was the town on its sunny slope,
and here were the hotel runners and the
custom house officers.   A deal of bustle,
a few tempers ruffled, a short sail on a
puffing tug, and we were ascending the
water-stairs to the Princess Hotel, in
Bermuda, and summer at last.

II.

FIRST IMPRESSIONS.

Our earliest impressions on landing were those of warmth, yet almost the first persons we spoke with said it was a chilly morning. The mercury then registered sixty degrees. Having settled ourselves leisurely in cozy rooms outlooking on the harbor and clustering islets, we penned a few lines to send by the home-going vessel, and started forth in search of the post office. As we turned toward the town we met several colored people, who saluted us as if we were old residents, and we began to feel at home at once. Several flannel-

clad young men were engaged in a game
of tennis on a court upon our right, and
the snow and the cold of the northland
became but a dream.   The highway
was hard, smooth and white.   The
cottages and villas we passed were
dazzling in the sun.   We saw roses and
geraniums in full bloom in the gardens,
and various other flowers whose names
we came gradually to know.   In one
garden the tall, graceful stalks of the
bamboo were waving in the soft breeze.

The roadway led us near the water's
edge, and beyond the pleasant shade of
the cedars we had glimpses of shifting
greens and blues that paled into light
shades near the shore.   Finally a turn
revealed a long, roofed wharf to which
the Trinidad was being moored by
means of huge cables.

Here was a crowd of loiterers—negroes,
native islanders and sojourners, who
were drawn thither by the diversion
offered by the unloading of the cargo.
As we wandered past, the captain was
shouting some orders from the bridge.
They have a curious way of fixing a
gangway in Bermuda.   The ship cannot

get very near the wharf, so two long beams are run out to her ; negroes slide along these and tie on cross-pieces by means of ropes ; then planks are laid down, and a safe means of communication with the shore established.

We walked along Front Street until we came to the first turning. All the stores are shaded by balconies, supported by small, square wooden pillars. These balconies in turn are protected by an extension of slanting roof. We noticed one very appropriate sign : " Trimming-ham & Co., Furnishings, etc."

Leaving Front Street, we climbed a somewhat steep ascent, and having hailed the first pedestrian whom we met, inquired the way to the post office. He did not appear to be going in our direction, but so politely offered to escort us that we could hardly refuse his kindly services. Our destination proved to be only a few steps, however, but our self-appointed guide saved us much trouble by informing us where we could obtain stamps for letters, the office being closed during the making up of the mail. It seemed odd to go to a grocery and wine and liquor store for postage stamps, yet we were evidently following the general custom. It is curious how almost every shop in Bermuda is like a country store. You are quite as likely to find confectionery in a shoe store, or jewelry in a furniture store, as in a shop where you would expect to see nothing but the article desired.

Boys, driving diminutive donkeys attached to diminutive carts, hailed us occasionally, entreating patronage. No one appeared to be in haste. There was a serenity and restfulness about the way the merchants seemed to be buying and selling, and we noticed on the faces of one and all an expression of placid contentment.

During our stroll about the town of Hamilton that first morning, we saw, floating from a flag-staff planted near a cosy cottage, a banner bearing a device of a wreath twined about a mitre :

"Mayhap there dwells his grace, the bishop," some one remarked, and the conjecture was correct, for on inquiry we were told that a wealthy lady had bequeathed the house and grounds

to the fortunate incumbent of the Bish-
opric of Newfoundland, who has under
his fatherly charge Bermuda, as well as
Labrador. He visits the former place
once in two years, remaining three
months. If there is as much diversity
in the characters of those whose heavenly
welfare he looks after, as there is in the
climates in which they dwell, his path
through life cannot be an easy one.
When in Bermuda a shiver must run
down and up his clerical spine every
time he thinks of the bleak coasts and
moorlands of the northern portion of his
spiritual domain.

It is surprising to note the luxuriant
vegetation that springs from Bermuda
soil.

Said a New York capitalist who had
made a prospecting tour among the
islands: "I don't think I'll invest here.
If I did they would be handing me over a
lot of rock with a few inches of ground
on it."

Of course in the valleys and reclaimed
marshes the soil is deeper than on the
hill slopes, and it is upon the low ground
that the best crops are raised. We

found the Easter lilies beginning to bloom in great wide fields and in small inclosures. The onion, in different stages of growth, was omnipresent. The life-plant, with its peculiar oval, pod-like bloom, early attracted our attention. The flowers of this plant are ordinarily known by the expressive but not euphonious name of "Floppers." Its leaves when plucked and put in moist earth will sprout young plants at each crenature.

The glare of sunlight on the white-washed walls and roofs of the houses proved for a time very trying to the eyes. The roofs are largely made of coral bricks laid longitudinally. Sometimes in excavating for a cellar enough coral rock will be taken out to build and roof the dwelling. Disused quarries may be seen in almost any part of the largest island.

The mechanic and mason do not thrive in Bermuda. We heard a gentleman say—one who had been an occasional visitor for twenty-five years—that he did not believe more than an average of one dwelling a year had been erected

during that space of time. From this
statement it may be truthfully surmised
that those structures which *have* been
erected have an air of stability. During
our Bermuda sojourn we saw but one
building on which laborers were working. This was Trinity Church, a fine
edifice, which is to replace the old house
of worship, destroyed some years since
by fire.

It is a popular notion that Bermuda is
the summit of a huge submarine mush-
room, and people are continually talking
about what will happen when the pedestal, or prop, breaks.

Among the objects naturally observed
on a first stroll through the streets of
Hamilton is the rubber-tree about which
the ever-jocular **Mr.** Clemens has made
some laughable comments. This tree,
which stands in the garden of a private
residence, sends out its huge limbs from
the trunk very near the earth ; and
under its shade, as we passed down
Queen's Street, an aged turbaned
negress, blacker than Erebus, had
paused. One tooth, like a rhinoceros'
tusk, protruded from her shrunken

254

found

stag
Th
p
a

III.

I the first walks we took wa to
th Shore. Having left sigtly
lamilton behind, we entere an
of cedars, where the over-arcing
s met and mingled above our
The air was spicy and the soft
in dreamy. We passed many ine
is as we wandered on. There was
odlawns, with its stately ties;
igle's Nest, perched high like an
rie; Dellwood, with its thick heges
f oleander, and Ocean Villa, with its
northwestern view commanding an unbroken stretch of sea. Strange and
beautiful wild flowers starred the ny-
side, delicate of hue and unique of fem.
The Bermuda blackbird (our catbrd)
was garrulous in the dense uner-
rowth. In a valley was a row of

257

mouth, and we hastened on lest she transfix us by some fateful spell. Doubtless she was perfectly harmless, but her visage was enough to give every soul in Bermuda the nightmare.

III.

THE NORTH SHORE AND SPANISH POINT.

ONE of the first walks we took was to the North Shore. Having left sightly Hotel Hamilton behind, we entered an avenue of cedars, where the over-arching boughs met and mingled above our heads. The air was spicy and the soft gloom dreamy. We passed many fine villas as we wandered on. There was Woodlawns, with its stately trees; Eagle's Nest, perched high like an eyrie; Dellwood, with its thick hedges of oleander, and Ocean Villa, with its northwestern view commanding an unbroken stretch of sea. Strange and beautiful wild flowers starred the wayside, delicate of hue and unique of form. The Bermuda blackbird (our catbird) was garrulous in the dense undergrowth. In a valley was a row of

257

twelve or fifteen banana trees. The corn was a foot in height. No house was so poor but that it could boast its plot of flowers. A woodpecker was drumming on the bough of a dead cedar, but he paid not the slightest heed to us as we paused under him.

Portions of the road to the North Shore led through cuttings in the coral rock fifteen, and, in some places, twenty feet in depth. Ferns were peeping from hollow and crevice. Of this lovely plant Bermuda has many varieties, and eight species of palms flourish. The roadway wall at the entrance to the grounds of the governor's house was aflame with the brilliant crimson of the bouganvillea. This climber blooms in the most lavish fashion, and offers a wealth of color that makes any garden a joy to look upon.

Half way between Hamilton and the North Shore is St. John's Evangelist, better known as Pembroke Church, with its not unattractive Norman tower. This edifice is painted buff, and is almost the hue of the highway, the tower being its only pleasant exterior feature;

what its interior may hold in the way
of interest I cannot say. The gateway
was securely barred, the wall was too
high to be scaled, and there was not a

soul within hailing distance. The grave-
yard that surrounds the church is set
with slabs of polished rock, beneath
which rest the good folk of past genera-
tions (and the evil, too, mayhap, if such
there ever were in Bermuda).

From a gentle eminence, reached after many windings, the ocean burst upon our sight through the lace-like boughs of the cedars. Near the beach the roadway branched and skirted the irregular coast east and west. We avoided a broken wall and clambered down the coral rock to a vantage point whence we could see, on the west, Ireland Island and its bristling fortifications, together with the tapering spars of the ships at its docks; and on the east, a long arm of land, dotted with white-roofed cottages. The water was an expanse of rippling sapphire. One ship, far at sea, seemed like a many-winged bird. The sun fell athwart her white sails, and they appeared as imperishable as marble. From our rocky perch we could count a dozen caves into which the tide surged, and made drowsy music with its ebb and flow. Two boys, seated upon a table-rock, their legs dangling twenty feet above the sea, chattered and cast their fishing lines. A negro laborer, in the far distance, was tossing up the matted seaweed from the beach. Seven hundred miles to the north and west lay home-land. It was winter there, but by no stretch of the imagination could we conjure up anything wintry here. The breeze had lulling hints of balm, and the sky was a blur of blue.

One afternoon, not long after the North Shore tramp, I started for Spanish Point with my friend, the Professor. At the very outset we filled our respective buttonholes with roadside nosegays. The day was one on which to make merry, and even the solitary goats, tethered here and there in deserted quarries, were evidently enjoying themselves. Pasturage is precious in Bermuda, and all graminivorous animals have to make the most of the scanty space their reach of rope allows them.

The people we met lounged along at a comfortable gait, as though it did not matter an atom when they reached their destination. Very likely they regarded the pace at which we strode by them as the sheerest folly in the world.

There was nothing about the Admiralty House and grounds that attracted us, but our curiosity was piqued at seeing a tall sheet-iron pipe rising above a

house that bore upon its entrance gate-
way the stately name of St. John's Hill.
Imagine our chagrin at being informed
that the place in question was a steam
laundry!—a steam laundry two miles
from town! Truly, time is no object
to the Bermudian.

As we approached the Point the wind
began to sweep in from the north, and
when we reached the rocks we sought a
sheltered spot where we could look off
across the bay undisturbed by the buffets
of the strong breeze. The tide was out,
and two negros and one white fisherman, were busy with their nets. The
latter was communicative, and con-
fided to us that the weather was very
bad for fishing ; but when we looked, as
we turned to leave, we found their large
cart nearly half filled with a fish not unlike the perch.

Through a small islet, just in front of
our secluded nook, the waves had worn
a passage, and this uneven archway
afforded us a charming water-vista. On
our left, a white silhouette on the azure
of the sky, towered the Gibb's Hill lighthouse. Opposite was Somerset Island,

263

while a projecting rock shut the dock-
yard from our view.

As we tramped along near the beach
on our homeward way, the Professor
saw a shining white and pink disc in the
sand. He charged upon it with his cane
"in rest," but it proved to be only a
jelly fish. Our greatest prize of the
afternoon was a huge ripe pawpaw, which
we purchased of a small colored girl,
for the exorbitant sum of two pence.

IV.

VARIOUS MATTERS MILITARY.

Owing to the rapid strides taken in naval and military science of late years, Bermuda is not the impregnable spot it once was considered. Notwithstanding this, it is still a powerful stronghold. But one regiment is at present stationed on the island (the 17th Leicestershire), and yet the red-coated soldiery are likely to appear at almost any turn.

265

They flash upon one unexpectedly in all their brilliancy of apparel. Young fellows they are, for the most part, strong and hardy-looking. We learned from the lieutenant on board the Trinidad, that Bermuda is not considered a desirable station. It is held to be altogether " slow," he said. The men, however, manage to divert themselves with cricket, tennis, boating, fishing, riding, and also with theatricals. We were told of a minstrel performance they gave, where one ambitious soloist tried to sing "Old Black Joe," and forgot both words and tune.

We heard the regimental band play one afternoon in the public gardens back of the Hamilton Hotel, and voted the performance a decided success. An open-air concert in mid-winter is indeed a novelty, and may be our applause was due to this fact rather than to the quality of the music. But we not only enjoyed the blended strains of the instruments, but also took much pleasure in watching the people who gathered to listen. There was quite a crowd within the garden, some pacing up and down the winding paths, some chatting in groups, some sitting on the benches beneath cedar and palm.

When the music ceased and the crowd dispersed we chanced to fall in with the gardener. A passing question in regard to some peculiar plant loosened his fluent tongue, and he ran on at an alarming rate. We did not know but that he would prove as bad as the " Ancient Mariner," although we had no wedding on hand. With us it was dinner.

But this gardener in his inconsequent way let fall some interesting bits of information. He went on at length in regard to the laziness of the negro, and he seemed to know whereof he spoke.

Of course, the officers of the garrison form an element not to be overlooked in the society of the island. What the balls given by families of standing would be without them one would scarcely venture to say ; and they have been known to enthrall the hearts of the visiting American, as well as of the local Bermudian, belles.

One sunny but breezy Saturday morning it came to my ears that there was to be a military display on the parade ground in the vicinity of Fort Hamilton and the garrison quarters, so thitherward I posted with all speed. There had been a severe squall the evening previous, but the only indications of a rainfall were the occasional pools in rocky indentations in the highway. The winding road led me through waving cedar groves, and finally brought me to a grassy, undulating space where the red-coated soldiers had already formed into line. Only a part of the regiment was under arms, but the men presented a picturesque appearance, their red coats contrasting vividly with the fresh green of the field. The band that had discoursed pleasing music in the garden the day before was in attendance, and now played more inspiring airs. Three officers, gallantly mounted, cantered to and fro with clanking of sabres, and the senior captain, who was then in command, shouted his orders in clarion tones.

The maneuvers of the troops were interesting, and were witnessed by a crowd of visitors who had driven to the scene in a variety of conveyances, and had gathered in friendly groups at several elevated points. After a series of marches and countermarches, arms were stacked, and the men formed an open hollow square, facing inward, the band occupying one side. Then, after a delay of some moments, the governor of the islands and his secretary came galloping over the crest of a flanking slope, and drew up in the rear of the band.

The commanding officer rode toward them and saluted, the music pealed, the men assumed statuesque poses, and began going through a kind of calisthenics, singing the while familiar popular airs. It was quite as good as an out-of-door opera, and vastly more entertaining. For half an hour every one, from the governor's wife and the trimly-clad English girls who accompanied her, down to the smallest donkey boy, was bent on the rhythmic swing of rising and falling arms. Then the men fell into compact line again, guns were shouldered and the troops, file by file, marched away towards the garrison.

"Right about face!" cried a voice

behind me, and my friend, the Professor, halted at my side with military precision. We grasped our canes and struck off upon a side road, where the bluebirds were twittering in the cedars, and showing now and then a flash of an azure wing that was like a detached scrap of sky.

As we descended into a little valley we found, quite isolated from all other buildings, a tiny one-storied structure, which bore the surprising sign, "American Bar."

"Thus are the garrison soldiers lured," said my companion.

V.

DRIVING TO ST. GEORGE'S.

IT chanced one Monday that four of us visited St. George's. Our driver was James and our steed, Belvidere. Two horses are rarely seen attached to a conveyance in Bermuda. We made a brave start along Front Street just as the ever-reliable colonel's watch announced half-past nine. The weather was as perfect as on a cloudless day of June in northern latitudes. The lively English sparrows, which have increased in number so rapidly on the islands, made the cedar groves vocal, and ever and anon a red bird darted like a tongue of flame across our way.

As far as Harrington's Sound we followed what is called the middle road. A few miles from Hamilton we paused a moment to have more than a passing glance at the picturesque old Devonshire Church, over which the ivy has reached its slender tendrils lovingly. In the churchyard is a venerable gnarled cedar tree, the oldest upon the islands, so report has it. Outside the church-yard on a convenient seat a negro was dozing away the early hours. The foliage was a brilliant green from recent rains. In one villa garden a large cala-bash tree hung full of the hard-shelled greenish oval fruit, which the natives pluck, dry, and shape into vessels for holding water. In the same garden were a pine-apple and mahogany tree. Morn-ing-glories in a riot of blossom were clambering over shrubs in the swamp land, and above these low reaches towered the graceful fan-palms.

Near a collection of cottages, known as Flat Village, we bore to the right and skirted the waters of Harrington Sound until we came to a deep inclosed pool near the shore, bearing the unattractive name of Devil's Hole. Here we de-scended, tipped the grinning negro guardian of the place, walked down some slippery steps, and beheld in thirty feet of pellucid water such a collection of fish as we had never before looked upon. They fairly swarmed. Hamlet, groupers and angel-fish they are called.

Think of angel-fish in the Devil's Hole! This last named species of the finny tribe merits its appellation. It is peculiar in shape, and when moving in the water flashes such rainbow blues and violets as are ravishing to the eye. The negro in charge was just feeding his captive family, and their greed was something disgusting. They tore piece-meal the small fish thrown in to them, and made the pool fairly boil in their frantic efforts to secure prey. There is a story told of an unlucky cur that ventured too near the edge of the hole, and met with a pitiful and untimely end, but I should hardly care to vouch for the truth of such a tale.

Just off the road which leads between Harrington Sound and Castle Harbor, Walsingham House is situated. This is the house where Thomas Moore dwelt during his stay upon the islands, and here is the famous calabash tree under which he is said to have composed some of his Bermudian poems. We found this tree in a sequestered spot—a fitting haunt for wooing the songful nine—and our guide nimbly scaled the boughs and procured a calabash for one of us.

Not far distant is one of the Walsing-ham caves. To reach this lovely grotto we clambered over and down irregular rocks, and stood on the shore of a tiny lake in which were mirrored the gleam-ing stalactites, for a slant sunbeam pierced the gloom and made such reflection possible. The clearness of the water was marvellous, and when our attendant lighted several dried cedar

boughs, the scene was like a glimpse of a veritable wonderland.

The glory of Walsingham House (if glory ever belonged to it) is a thing of

the past. It is unoccupied to-day save
by the spiders, and the air of desolation
that clings about the place would make
even the happy-hearted Tom Moore
melancholy, could he come back from
spirit-land and view his whilom residence.

After leaving Walsingham, Belvidere
was put through his paces. We dashed
across the long causeway that connects
the mainland (as the largest island is
often called) and Long Bird Island.
The water of Castle Harbor presented a
panorama of shifting hues. Near shore it
was the softest, most delicate green ;
above the reefs it was steely gray, and
beyond the blue shaded into the deepest
indigo.

Far on our right, notching the horizon,
were various rocks and islands, promi-
nent among them Castle Island, on
which are the ruins of a once massive
fortification. In the halcyon days of the
Spanish main, Castle Harbor is said to
have been a favorite resort of those free
sea rovers, the buccaneers ; and many
are the tales, so rumor saith, that its
coves and isles might tell of them. And

as for Castle Island's sturdy, long-coated soldiers, and the frilled and be-laced officers, who once passed and re-passed along the corridors of its forts and its deserted paths, not so much as a lonely wraith ever wanders back, at least to mortal knowledge.

A second causeway and an iron draw-bridge connect Long Bird Island and St. Geoge's, and ere long we found our-selves dashing down the narrow streets of the little, white, old sleepy town. Ever since the residence of the governor was removed to Hamilton, St. George's has been in a dream of days that were. One solitary red-coat was striding across the market square when we drew up in front of a hotel bearing the same name as the town. There was a row of shops on the lower story, and we reached the inn proper by a winding flight of stairs at one corner of the building. What a funny little place it was!—and is now ; you will say so if you go to visit it. The prints upon the wall will take you back fifty years, and there are things that will remove you still further from the present.

The landlord ought to be a good man, for his name is Virtue. Some one remarked, on paying him an extraordinary price for a very ordinary dinner, that "virtue was not his only reward."

There are several forts at St. George's, but civilians are not allowed to visit them. One may wander in the public gardens, and sit in the shade of date palms more than one hundred and fifty years old. Here is to be seen the monument to Sir George Somers, after whom the town is named. A bluff old fellow and a brave one was Sir George. Shipwrecked here in 1609, with some colonists bound for Virginia, he constructed two vessels of cedar, and with them sailed to Jamestown. Finding that colony in a destitute condition he volunteered to return to the islands for assistance. Buffeted far to the north by storms, he at last succeeded in reaching his destination, only to die from exposure and privation.

The oldest church on the island is St. Peter's at St. George's. It certainly is not an attractive structure, and aside from the ancient communion service and the baptismal font, contains nothing of interest. But the churchyard that sur-rounds it is a spot to dream in. We found many roses blooming in the deep grass, and there were odd, half-effaced inscriptions on many of the tombstones.

At mid-afternoon we turned our faces toward Hamilton. We were bowling along at a rapid pace when our driver whirled us into a yard and drew up some distance in the rear of a rough cottage.

"Why tarry here?" we inquired.

"More caves to see," said James.

But before plunging again into "under-earth" we plucked jasmine and peach blossoms and stood beneath a curious screw-palm tree.

Joice's caves are called the Island cave and Queen's cave; the former name is given because the cave contains a tiny islet in a tiny lake, the latter because at some time certain members of the royal family have deigned to set foot in it. We managed to procure several very beautiful pieces of stalactite in Queen's cave, into which we climbed for a long distance, until we were half choked by the combined smoke from burnt cedar boughs and candles, when we decided that there was nothing romantic in cavern exploring, and hastily retreated to the outer air.

Yet we were by no means sorry to have seen Joice's caves. They have their distinctive features, and the visitor to Bermuda should not be beguiled into thinking that if he has visited the Walsingham cavern he has exhausted the underground beauties of the island.

When the artificial light flared up in the Island cave and suddenly threw before us the crystalline sheet of water, the gleaming stalactites above reproduced below, and the rugged oval mass in the center of the pool, a cry of surprise and delight rose from our lips involuntarily. It was one of the not-to-be-forgotten pictures.

Through the breezy hours of late afternoon we sped over the North Shore road ; past Gallows Island, where once in the long ago a slave was hung ; past the Wells, whence the navy once procured its water supply ; past Gibbins Bay, where high tide prevented us from gathering the curiously-shaped shells, and past " Ducking Stool " rock, where island-scolds and witches were once soused in the waves.

From my western window that evening I saw the full glory of a Bermudian sunset. The water flashed, the islands glowed, and the sky—oh ! the sky flamed and burned in a thousand slender spires, and then how softly dusk fell, while the crescent moon showed its silver blade !

VI.

IRELAND ISLAND AND GIBB'S HILL.

Twice a day regularly, and sometimes oftener, the steam yacht Moondyne runs from Hamilton to Ireland Island. In order to visit the island, the floating dock and the ships, considerable red-tape must be encountered. You are obliged to fill out a printed application and send it to the captain in charge. This is a simple matter of form, for no one is ever denied permission. The application is returned with the officer's signature, and, armed with one, we boarded the Moondyne. The steamer held a sinuous course between various islands of the three hundred and sixty-five that constitute the Bermuda group, touched at Boaz Island with its reminiscences of the convict settlement, and landed within the dockyard. We filed to the guardhouse and presented our "open sesame"; we subscribed our names and residences in a well-filled register and then awaited the pleasure of a blue-uniformed official in a vizored cap. He had an eccentric gait and a gruff voice, and he had to be "thawed" with a certain disc bearing the image of good Queen Victoria, before he became communicative.

We "did" the place thoroughly. First was the floating dock where the gun-boats, Vixen and Viper, were undergoing repairs. This dock, which was brought across the Atlantic in 1868, is still said to be the largest of its kind in the world. It resembles more than anything else a huge deckless ship with bow and stern cut square off. The hammering and scraping that were going on here bore no comparison to the noises which fairly deafened us in the various shops we visited. From these we emerged feeling as though we should be grateful for new organs of hearing. We were permitted to descend to the gun-deck, and to crawl into one of the turrets of the gunboat Scorpion, a difficult undertaking, as we found iron and steel did not readily yield when brought into forcible contact with the cranium.

On the whole, Ireland Island did not please us. It had a worn-out, useless appearance. There were a few rusty torpedo boats about that looked like gigantic crabs. The workmen in the shops were apathetic. The marines moved with lazy abandon. Nothing recalled to mind England's proud claim to be " mistress of the seas " save the old five-deck, line-of-battle ship, the Irresistible, which was with Nelson at the

Nile and Trafalgar. This hoary veteran is used as a lodging place and mess-room for the dock-yard laborers, and the sight of her somehow inspires one.

On the highest point of land in Bermuda Gibb's Hill lighthouse is situated, and no one should leave the islands without climbing its tower. The road to Gibb's Hill leads around the head of the harbor, past the garden, where stand the five stately royal palms, whose trunks have the appearance of smoothly-carven, polished granite. On the left is the house occupied by the Princess Louise during her visit to Bermuda—a red-letter year in island annals. On the way to the lighthouse one may visit the pretty Gothic church at Paget, and the sand banks which the wind has cast up from the south shore, burying all, save a crumbling chimney of one of the early-time houses.

Pleasant villas succeed one another, and the blue water-reaches are never for many moments lost to view. It was clear and calm when we started for the hill, but the wind suddenly veered and blew up, from some unknown misty nook of the Atlantic, rain clouds that gave us occasional dashes, and by the time we had wound up and up to the lighthouse tower, in the upper air all the trumpets of the sky were sounding their alarm. We climbed one hundred and thirty-three feet of spiral stairs, while the hollow, tapering pillar of iron trembled and quivered beneath the force of the gale. The waves were angry on the reefs, and through frequent rifts in the wind-driven clouds nearly all the islands, save remote St. George's and St. David's, caught a momentary brightening ray of sunlight.

VII.

L'ENVOI.

WHEN Juan Bermudez, commanding the ship La Garza, discovered the islands that bear his name in 1515, he little realized what a blessing they would be in after time to frail dwellers in chilly northern climes. People who have sought the world over for an equable climate have found it at last here. However let no one be deceived into thinking that Bermuda weather is perfection. It has its little eccentricities that have to be put up with, but one may depend that the mercury will never drop below fifty, and even in the summer will not rise above eighty-five. One may be sure, too, that if rain does fall it will not continue to do so long, and when a storm has ceased that the moisture will disappear from the earth as if it were merely dew.

The wind has been known to blow from every point of the compass in the space of two hours, but it makes no practice of cutting such unseemly capers. So you who are weary of wintry days, of snow and sleet and ice; you who have felt the wasting hand of disease and would be rejuvenated; you who long for sweet, bracing, yet balmy air, air that rarely chills; you who love life under the open skies, turn your faces toward the " summer isles." What matter if the sea be sometimes rough? A few hours of sea-sickness can be endured, and the joy of recovery will recompense you should you experience the indescribable sensation.

In these hap-hazard records of a Bermudian sojourn very many things have been left unsaid. There has been little attempt to go into matters historical. With good guide books at command one may post one's self thoroughly in regard to the limited history of the islands and their various sights, but no book, no description, howsoever vivid, can convey to the mind the charm of Bermuda.

Of our variqus excursions by water, in row and sail boats, I have not spoken ; how we went " reefing," and saw the lovely sea-anemones, and gathered curiosities from beneath the waves. How, in the governor's grounds at Mt. Langton, we strolled about among the curious plants, I have not told ; nor how we crossed one Sunday afternoon by private ferry, and went to hear the bishop preach in Paget church ; nor how we climbed through cedar groves upon the south shore to find the rock whereon Ferdinand Camelo, one of the first mariners to sail Bermudian waters, engraved an inscription and date ; nor yet of our pilgrimage to the natural arch at Tucker's Town.

The Bermudian journal must be closed ; we must say farewell to the lovely isles that Waller sang of, and Montgomery and Moore. To the " still-vexed Bermoothes "of Ariel and Prospero, adieu !

See ! the cables are being cast off. The bow of the Trinidad is swinging from the wharf. One last wave of the hand

to the palms and the cedars, to the Princess Hotel on the harbor shore, to the
Hamilton down-looking on the town, to
the forts and the red-coated soldiers,
and to the newly-made friends we leave
behind. Good-bye to the happy " summer isles."

Re-tune the lyre, and sweep the quivering
  strings,
  For of the isles where Spring is always young
And Summer rests with ever-folded wings,
  Shall one more song be sung !

To him who roams their hills and valleys wild,
  Caressed by all the wooing airs that blow,
They seem an ocean-eden undefiled
  That never dreamed of woe.

Year-long the minstrels of the woodland-close
  Are jubilant within the boughs above,—
Year-long unfolds the crimson-hearted rose
  That plighted lovers love.

To fair perfection swells the luscious fruit,
  Nor fears the wan and withering touch of
    cold ;
The waves resound as does a mighty lute
  Whose strains are never old.

And in the calm, sequestered coral coves,
  Clear depths reveal, where prismy lights flash
    free,
Enrapturing visions of the shadowy groves
  Of cavernous under-sea.

Brim me yon carved and polished calabash,
  And I will pledge, as high the cup I raise,
Fond memories, that no fire can burn to ash,
  Of bland Bermudian days.

Lightning Source UK Ltd.
Milton Keynes UK
UKHW022123211118
332759UK00018B/1851/P